THE BULLDOGGERS CLUB

THE TALE OF THE
ILL-GOTTEN CATFISH

THE BULLDOGGERS SERIES
BOOK 1

BARBARA HAY

THE ROADRUNNER PRESS
OKLAHOMA CITY

Published by The RoadRunner Press
Oklahoma City
www.TheRoadRunnerPress.com

First edition hardcover, The RoadRunner Press, October 2012
Printed in the United States of America.
Cover Illustration: Tim Jessell
Interior Illustrations: Steven Walker
Map by Steven Walker
Cover design by Steven Walker

Will Rogers quote originally published in the New York Times,
among other papers in syndication, on 17 August 1924. Used with
permission of the Will Rogers Memorial Museum, Claremore, Okla.

Published October 16, 2012

Manufactured by Thomson-Shore, Dexter, MI (USA) / RMA584DR512, September, 2012

Library of Congress Control Number: 2012939713

Publisher's Cataloging-In-Publication Data
(Prepared by The Donohue Group, Inc.)

Hay, Barbara.
   The tale of the ill-gotten catfish / Barbara Hay. -- 1st ed.

   p. : ill., map ; cm. -- (The Bulldoggers Club ; Bk.1)

   Summary: A group of boys form a kids' outdoor activities club. When they
go fishing, bullies force them to fish in a neighbor's pond that is off limits. Their
troubles build, but, in the end, the boys learn about honesty and friendship.
   ISBN: 978-1-937054-15-1 (hardcover)

   1. Boys--Societies and clubs--Juvenile fiction. 2. Fishing--Juvenile fiction. 3.
Truthfulness and falsehood--Juvenile fiction. 4. Boys--Fiction. 5. Clubs--Fiction.
6. Fishing--Fiction. 7. Honesty--Fiction. I. Title.

PZ7.H31382 Tal 2012
[Fic]   2012939713

For Peter

"A man that don't love a horse,
there is something the matter with him."

— Will Rogers,
Oklahoma humorist
(1879 - 1935)

THE BULLDOGGERS CLUB

The Tale of the
Ill-Gotten Catfish

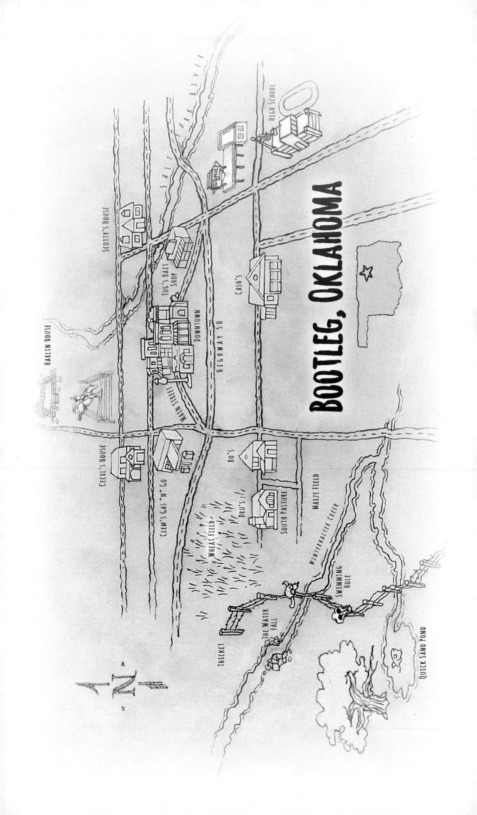

Chapter 1
The Winterhalters

I WOKE TO OKLAHOMA SUNSHINE blasting, like a blow
torch, through my window and Kevin screaming "Doodoo" in
my ear. *Would the kid ever learn to say my name right*, I wondered.
I rolled over and pulled the pillow over my head to block out the
noise coming from my baby brother and the sunbeams bearing
down through my bedroom window.

"Doodoo!" Kevin shouted, louder if that's possible.

The only way to make him stop was to get out of bed, even
though it was Saturday and by rights I could have slept in. I sat up
and pulled my blanket around me, like a cape. It was the beginning of May, but the early morning air was chilly and the wood
floor was cold.

Kevin had already sensed my surrender. He toddled over and
dropped my slippers in my lap.

"Sippers," he said.

How could a guy stay mad? I tousled the red curls on his head. He
grinned and I grinned back. I had just about gotten over being

called "Doodoo" when Mom hollered from the kitchen.

"Dru, you up?"

"Yup," I called back.

"Could you please keep an eye on Kevin while I run your dad's coffee to the barn."

"Do I have to?"

"Yes, you have to."

For now, little brother was quietly playing with a pile of wooden blocks on the braided rug by my bed. Kevin accounted for, I turned and looked for some clothes to put on. My jeans hung on the chair by my desk. I grabbed them, slid my legs in, and pulled a camouflage T-shirt from the dresser drawer. When I turned back around, Kevin was gone.

I headed for the kitchen.

"Kev, where'd you go?"

The question was no more out of my mouth when I heard the screen door slam. I figured it was Mom leaving. I heaved a big sigh and began checking Kevin's favorite hiding spots: Behind the television set in the living room. No Kevin. Under the dining room table. Nope, not there, either. Just to be thorough, I gave a shout through the screen door at the back porch.

"Kee-viiiii-nnn."

"Yup," Kevin answered.

His answer came from outside. I traded my slippers for my boots, grabbed my cowboy hat off the peg by the back door, and headed in the direction of his voice.

"What are you doing?" I hollered, trying to get a bearing on his exact location.

"Eatin' 'cans."

" 'Cans" is Kevin-speak for "pecans." I walked around the side of the house, listening, trying to think where there still might be pecans on the ground that the squirrels hadn't found.

"What *are* you doing?" I asked again.

Then I saw him. He was standing by the rabbit hutch.

"Eatin' 'cans." He said between chews.

His back was to me, and I had a sinking feeling in my stomach as I ran over to him.

"Stop eating those! Those aren't 'cans. They're rabbit poop!"

I peeled open his fist and brushed the remaining black droppings to the ground: "Oh, that's gross."

Kevin looked up at me, scared. His face clouded over and his bottom lip quivered. Tears the size of marbles popped out of his eyes and rolled down his cheeks. He let out a loud wail, loud enough to make Mom run the rest of the way from the barn, probably convinced I was skinning him alive.

"What's going on?" Mom asked, taking in the situation with one swift glance. She bent down, stuck a finger in Kevin's mouth, and dug out the last, now mushy, 'cans.

"He ran outside after you," I said.

"I told you to watch him."

"I did. That's how come he's crying."

She took a deep breath. I could tell she was fighting to keep her temper. "First of all, watch how you talk to me, young man. And second, this isn't the first time he's gotten away from you, Dru. You are almost thirteen years old, old enough to know just how dangerous a ranch can be, especially for a three-year-old. Remember that little boy who drowned last summer in the horse trough? His mother and father were right there. It can happen so fast."

Tears wet the corners of her eyes, and I could tell she was imagining how those parents must have felt when they found their lifeless son facedown in the water. She cleared her throat, brushed her eyes with the backs of her hands, and turned her attention back to me.

"When you finish breakfast you can pull the dandelions and mow the front yard. And when you get done with that, you can pull the weeds in the pumpkin patch. That should give you plenty of time to think about what it means to be responsible and what you've done wrong today."

She took Kevin by the hand and led him inside, fussing at him for putting such nasty things in his mouth.

I headed for the barn. The list of chores she had asked me to do were a lot worse than anything I had done to Kevin, but all the while a voice in my head also kept saying, *I should have been more careful with Kevin.*

The barn door slid open with one pull, and I stepped into the shadows, walked past the stalls to the other end of the barn, and slid open another door. Checkers, my quarter horse, stood under the scrub cedar at the far end of our small pasture. He's called a quarter horse because that's his breed, or the kind of horse he is, not because he's one-fourth horse or anything like that. Seems the British brought their horses over here to America, bred them with the Spaniards' horses, and then raced them on quarter-mile tracks. That's how they got their name: American Quarter Horse. To this day, there isn't nothing faster on the quarter-mile.

Just about everybody I know around here rides quarter horses because of their grit, their speed, and their ability to read a steer's mind. Checkers is as much a part of the family as anyone. I raised him from a foal, even helped to break him to the saddle, but I can't take all the credit. My dad trained him to be a roping horse, and I think Checkers might know more about roping than I do.

At the sight of me, Checkers's ears pricked up and he trotted towards the barn. The rest of the horses followed him. I opened the doors on four stalls and, as the horses went in, I closed the doors behind them one by one. I filled a bucket with rolled oats, using a coffee can to give each horse a serving. The smell of the oats made my stomach growl with hunger, but I had a feeling it was a little too soon to return to the house—better to give Mom time to cool off before facing her again.

Instead, I headed to the tack room, where we house our gear: saddle blankets, ropes, bridles, bits. We keep our chaps there, too.

I found Dad there, rubbing down the saddles with a soft rag dipped in Neatsfoot oil.

4

"What's all the commotion about?" He didn't bother to look up from what he was doing as he asked.

"Nothing."

I fiddled with the fringe on the Western saddle he was working on, but if I thought my morning slipup had gone unnoticed I was wrong.

"I remember when you were Kevin's age and your poor Mom about lost her wits every time you were out of her sight."

"The guys and I were planning to go fishing," I said, in an effort to change the subject. "After I get my chores done."

He didn't need to say anything more; I already felt bad enough. And, with all the extra chores mom had assigned me, I would be lucky to go fishing at all, Saturday or not.

"The usual place?" Dad asked as he stood to put up the rag and oil on one of the plank shelves.

"Down by the swimming hole," I said.

The sound of mom ringing the cowbell on the front porch cut me off. Dad led the way out of the tack room.

"Breakfast is ready."

Chapter 2
The Bulldoggers Club

AFTER I FINISHED MY breakfast, I knew I would have to work fast, because we were having a Bulldoggers Club meeting, and the other three members—Bo, Cecil, and Scotty—were due to arrive shortly after noon. We planned to discuss the junior roping event coming up in a week's time, over a little fishing.

Since it was my idea to name us The Bulldoggers Club, I am the president. We gave ourselves official offices and titles so folks would know we are serious about rodeo. Kids don't always get taken serious about stuff, you know.

Here in Bootleg, Oklahoma, everybody works cattle, or raises horses, or works the land in one way or another. Roping and riding come with the territory.

Rodeo, you could say, is mainly about making fun out of the hard work it takes to keep a ranch running. There is always some reason to be rounding up cattle, whether it is springtime when we cull and sort the herd or fall when we are getting ready to go to the stockyard sale. Year-round, we get a lot of practice roping steers and riding horses as part of daily life in Bootleg.

My dad says that we Winterhalters have been ranching this land since the days when the first settlers came to these parts, and that would be more than a hundred years ago. My great-granddaddy, Gunther Winterhalter, hiked clear across Germany to England and hitched himself a ride on a ship that was sailing for America way back in 1893. He had heard they were giving away free land to anyone tough enough to make a go of it, and we have been here ever since.

By the time my buddy Bo rode up the lane, I had pulled the dandelions, mowed, and was almost done weeding the pumpkin patch.

"Hey Dru. Where's Cecil and Scotty?" He asked as he swung down off Ranger's back and tied him to a fence post.

"They should be here soon," I said.

Bo took one look at what I was doing and pitched in to help me finish pulling the last few weeds. I had been putting them in a wheelbarrow. Bo grabbed its handles and wheeled it over to what was fast becoming a good-size brush pile, a short piece away from the barn. The brush pile had last been burned in December, after a big snow. Bo, Cecil, Scotty, and I had taken turns watching it so the fire wouldn't get out of hand. Five months later it still smelled like charcoal.

Bo and I have lived next door to each other since the day we were born: July fourth. (He's two hours older than me; something he never lets me forget.) His horse, Ranger, and my horse are also twins, so we figure we're related in a strange cosmic sort of way.

Bo's sort of a history buff, being that his great-grandpa came here as a freed slave after the Civil War and found work on Melbourne "Bootleg" Harlin's Ranch. The famous African-American-Cherokee rodeo cowboy Bill Pickett worked alongside Bo's great-grandpa, rounding up cattle, breaking horses for riding, and whatnot. Pickett's father, Tom, was born a slave, too.

7

Bill Pickett is credited with inventing bulldogging, or steer wrestling. They say he bit the lip of steers to bring them down and that he got the idea from watching dogs do the same thing when herding wayward cattle on the range. Pickett would bite a big ol' steer's bottom lip with his teeth and wouldn't let go until the steer laid down. Pickett's bite-'em style made him a legend in rodeo circles. Though lip biting is a no-no in the modern arena, according to Bo.

Bo loves roping and riding and the taste of dust in his teeth, but since his dad took a fall from a bull at the Bear Creek Rodeo, he has been busier than a one-armed hog-tier trying to keep up with chores around their place. He reminded me of those broncos at the rodeo just before a run, twisting and snorting and chomping at the bit to get the show on the road.

Bo was acting that way now as we waited for the other two Bulldoggers to arrive. Luckily, I saw Cecil come galloping up on Rocket as we came back from stowing the wheelbarrow in the tool shed. Rocket is part thoroughbred and part quarter horse and runs like, well, a rocket.

Cecil was off Rocket before he came to a stop. He tied him up to the fence and sidled over to us, fishing pole in hand.

"Hey," he said, with a friendly nod.

"We're waiting for Scotty," I said.

Cecil Rill is vice president of The Bulldoggers Club. He moved to Bootleg when he was five. He lives on a wheat farm with his grandma and two of his uncles a mile or so north of Winterhalter Creek. He is shorter than I am but stocky and sure-footed, and he can throw a rope and hit any target, moving or not.

When his mom ran off with his dad's best friend, his father couldn't take care of him and work his shift at the oil refinery in Bear Creek, so his grandma said, "Come on and live with me and I'll take good care of you." As far as I know, she's done just like she promised.

Before I introduce you to any of our other members, I guess

The Bulldoggers Club

I should explain exactly what we do in The Bulldoggers Club, for those who have never heard of us or our club before.

Basically we are a bunch of guys who like to ride horses and like to rodeo. Bulldogging is a rodeo event that calls for a cowboy to jump from his horse, grab a steer by the horns, and flip him onto the ground—the faster the better.

Unfortunately, none of my fellow Bulldoggers or myself are old enough yet to compete in the rodeo's bulldogging competition, but we all agreed that "The Calf Ropers Club" didn't sound half as cool as "The Bulldoggers Club."

Bo says we're carrying on history. Back in the 1700s, bulldogging literally meant working cattle with bulldogs. Yep, the dogs were trained to drive cattle and guard stock. An experienced eighty-pound bulldog could topple an eighteen-hundred pound bull—and that's no easy feat.

In the United States, cowboy contests have been around since the 1820s, but bulldogging dates to 1903 when Bill Pickett supposedly laid down that ornery longhorn.

Bo's told us a lot about rodeo history, but I'll spare you the lesson since this is no classroom.

Anyway I could tell Cecil and Bo were getting antsy.

The weather looked right for hooking fish, but in Oklahoma there was no guarantee that it would stay that way. The last weather report I had heard had storms headed our way in the next few days.

Fish get awful hungry right before a storm.

Might turn out to be a decent afternoon, after all.

Chapter 3
The Two Biggest Jerks in Bootleg

AS MEMBERS OF THE Bulldoggers Club, we spend a lot of time swinging lariats, and it doesn't matter exactly what we aim for, so long as we hit it. They tell of cowboys who roped mice, bears, wives, and geese, but today we had to settle for an old stump.

Waiting for Scotty to arrive, Bo and Cecil and I took turns tossing our catch-ropes, not saying much. I suspect we were all thinking about the same thing: Fishing.

Our poles were leaned against the fence just begging us to grab them up and go.

"What's taking Scotty so long?" Bo asked, after he had lassoed the old hollowed-out tree stump for about the hundredth time.

"I'll give him a call."

Cecil pulled a cell phone from his shirt pocket and dialed Scotty's number. Cecil's dad had given him the phone to ease his grandma's mind during times like this when we were out of yelling distance.

While Cecil dialed, I sized up the tree stump, swung my rope, and missed. Maybe my mind was more on fishing than roping.

"Scotty's grandma says he's on his way," Cecil said.

Cecil had no more closed his phone and turned to face the stump, when off in the distance a cloud of dust appeared headed our way. It was Scotty on Paint. He was riding at a full gallop.

"That was quick," I said.

Cecil and Bo laughed. Scotty swung his hat in the air over his head in a silent hello. Scotty Fender, cowboy and whiz kid. Scotty is the only guy I have ever known who can whip through math tests like a professor and ride a horse like an old cowhand. His horse of choice is a pinto named Paint. Paint really looks as if someone splashed big drops of brown paint on his white coat.

The youngest of seven boys, Scotty lives on the other side of Bootleg, near Salt Fork River. Most of his brothers are grown with wives and kids of their own. His folks run what used to be known as Fender's Lodge, but now that folks from the city want to vacation at a real working cattle ranch, they call it Fender's Guest Ranch. My dad says we have to keep changing with the times, and nowadays many ranchers have to take a job in town or find a new way to make their ranch pay if they want to keep their ranch—it takes a lot of cash money to keep the trucks and tractors in diesel fuel and to pay the hired hands.

As for me, I hang out at Scotty's for two reasons: One, Mrs. Fender always has freshly made cinnamon rolls, with runny icing that drips on your chin when you eat them, in the morning. Mm-mmm. And two, his dad was a world champion rodeo rider. I never tire of listening to the stories he tells, or eating cinnamon rolls.

"Hey," Scotty said to us, when he got close enough.

He swung down out of the saddle with his fishing pole gripped in his hand. He wrapped Paint's reins through the fence rail near the water trough, loose enough for him to be able to take a drink.

"Sorry I'm late," he said, out of breath, as if he himself had run the five miles from his house to mine, instead of Paint. "I was helping round up cattle that broke through the fence last night."

"No big deal," I said.

Cecil and Bo both shrugged an okay—we'd all been there. Life on a ranch is nothing if not a series of daily emergencies. That is why you had to take time off when you could get it. With fishing poles and tackle boxes in hand we set off across the south pasture to our regular fishing spot.

The afternoon sun was high overhead as we made our way across the crunchy chewed-to-the-nub grass. The cattle that had been grazing on this acreage had been moved to another pasture.

Ranching is done differently than it was in the Wild West days. Some people no longer own land; instead they lease it from somebody else and put cattle on it to graze and grow fat. They get paid for the gain, or the weight each steer gains over the summer or the winter. Other folks operate cow-calf operations, breeding cows then selling off the calves when they come along. And quite a few families, like Bo's and mine, live on small ranches—maybe two hundred to three hundred acres, work about twenty to thirty head of cattle, and have someone holding down a day job, like my Dad, who works in the agriculture department at the local university.

The day was fast slipping away, as we hurried over the far fence, hiked down to the creek bed, and walked along the smooth rocks poking their heads above the slow-moving stream. Cecil and Bo took turns pushing each other off the rocks and into the cold water, then scrambling back up and going a few more steps before repeating the process all over again. They were making so much racket I didn't hear the voices until we got to where the creek bed widens and the stream water deepens several feet.

That's when we saw them. And they saw us.

"Weasel Jack and Bart the Buffoon at twelve o'clock," Scotty said in a stage whisper.

It could have gone either way, but when Jack and Bart stood to get a better look at us, I knew we were in trouble. They were not called "The Two Biggest Jerks in Bootleg" for nothing.

Chapter 4
Four Big Chickens

JACK AND BART ARE WELL known in our town for scaring kids into surrendering just about anything these two might get a hankering for, rather than suffering the wrath of Jack and Bart. Though come to think of it, the last time I had a run-in with them, I gave them my lunch money and they still chased me clear to Lucy's Cafe. If it hadn't been for Mr. LeRoy I would still be running. He stepped out of the cafe door just as I came flying by. I guess he figured out what was what, because he greeted me like I was supposed to be meeting him there, and Jack and Bart slunk off without a word.

Not that I am chicken or anything, but those two weigh more than the four of us put together. Common sense would tell anybody, except maybe Cecil, to avoid such no-goods.

"Oh look," Jack said to Bart, "it's a flock of hicks."

"I think these rodeo clowns are spying on us, Jack." Bart the Buffoon lumbered toward us. "Or were you guys maybe planning to fish here?"

We all spoke at the same time.

"No," Cecil and Bo said.

"Yes," Scotty and I said.

"You sound like a bunch of girls trying to make up your minds," Jack said.

"Just a bunch of runts," Bart said.

As they drew closer, Cecil pulled a long thin piece of straw through his crooked front teeth, then stuck it behind his ear. I took it as a very bad sign of things to come.

What most folks don't know about Cecil is that he has a temper. I think it has to do with his mom running off, but I could be wrong. I was just waiting for one of those two knuckleheads to make him mad, because despite his small size, if Cecil gets pushed too far, it's hard to tell what might happen next. I once saw him lose his temper outside our sixth-grade classroom when Clay Ramey, an eighth-grader, tried to take away a fourth-grader's lunch. Let's just say there were sandwich guts everywhere before it was all over, and Cecil almost got suspended from school.

This was a different situation. Jack and Bart weren't eighth-graders. They were football players at Bootleg High School. And they weren't supposed to be smoking.

Bart caught me staring at his cigarette, and I thought I was a goner. He stalked over to me and knocked his ashes onto my sneakers, as if it was okay for him to be smoking and he didn't care who knew about it. But I had heard Scotty's older brother, Reggie, talking about how tough on smoking the new football coach was. Last week he made some guys run laps for the whole two hours of practice when he found out they had been smoking.

"You still on the football team?" I heard myself asking, looking right at the hand that held that cigarette. I couldn't believe it was me saying those words. *I am going to get kilt*, I thought.

"What's it to you," Bart said. He drew a long puff from his cigarette, coughed, and spewed stinky smoke in my face.

Cecil stepped up next to me.

"You won't be if Coach Brown catches you smoking,"

"That ol' rat's tail can't run fast enough," Bart said.

Jack laughed and gave his partner-in-crime a fist bump.

"He won't catch us, unless someone tells him we was smoking." Bart gave each of us a good hard look. "Anyone feel like snitching?"

The four of us shook our heads back and forth, like the chickens we were.

"Not us," I said. "That is, as long as we get to fish here, I mean."

Where was I coming up with this stuff? Words just kept bypassing my brain and popping out of my mouth uncensored.

"You trying to make a deal with me?" Bart asked, and he smiled again. "I'll tell you what . . ."

He walked up real close to me, so close I could smell the stink of cigarette smoke and pizza on his breath. I gave Cecil, Bo, and Scotty a weak smile, thinking *maybe these guys aren't so bad, after all.*

"Here's the deal," Bart said. "You can fish here, all right, over my dead body."

Then he growled at me, like a mountain lion or a Bengal tiger from the zoo or a black bear—I couldn't quite place the roar. I was too shaken up.

All I know is we started running. We ran across Winterhalter Creek and up the other bank, scrambling for handholds on tree roots sticking from the dirt. We ran across the hay meadow and into our neighbor's field of maize, following the rows spaced three feet apart and straight as arrows as far as we could see. We ran as if our lives depended on it, which I pretty much think they did.

The last I saw of Jack and Bart, they stood at the edge of the hay meadow, holding their sides, laughing.

Chapter 5
Quicksand

"NOW WHAT DO WE DO?" Bo asked. We were walking in the ditch along the maize field, single file, heading west. "We're running out of time to fish."

Bo was always worrying about the time, afraid of getting home late, but then if my dad was laid up like his was, I would probably worry if he was home all by himself for too long, too.

Cecil piped up from in front.

"We could cut back across to the creek, farther up. Those boneheads are too lazy to go that far."

"What about Quicksand Pond?" Scotty asked, knowing full well what our response would be.

"Oh, yeah," I said. "If we don't sink to our deaths, that old witch will have us for dinner."

I was, of course, referring to The Witch of Bootleg, also known as Nurse Blanchett. She was the school nurse during my dad's school days. Now, from what I could tell, she spent her time growing weird weeds and medicinal herbs, hunched over a kettle

in her backyard brewing horrible concoctions I could smell at my house, if the wind blew right.

"I heard she went to Oklahoma City to nurse her sister," Scotty said, but his voice lacked conviction.

Nurse Blanchett's place came into view.

"We could check it out," I said. "See if she has anything brewing—that'd be a sure sign if she was home."

We set off across through the tall grass towards her sandstone house. My dad says it must have been built in the Stone Age, it is so old; my mom thinks it should be on the historic registry. I'm convinced the old place is haunted. The outbuildings behind her house have more out than in. As the house came in view, we dropped to our stomachs, like infantrymen inching towards a target. We continued edging nearer until we reached the barbed wire fence. The old witch had hung cattle skulls and huge dead catfish heads on the dry-rotted posts to ward off intruders. It nearly worked on us, but then we caught sight of the pond and the lure of it was more powerful than the fear.

"I don't see any smoke," Bo said.

We climbed over the rusted barbed wire fence careful not to catch ourselves or hang up our fishing gear. As we crept through thistles and prickly pear and hid behind the cottonwoods that dotted the field, I could see a mess of cats sleeping in the shade of the back porch. They looked like woolly caterpillars from this distance.

Once it seemed certain Nurse Blanchett wasn't home, we made a beeline for her pond, running and jumping in our excitement.

While I couldn't wait to bait my hook, I was, nonetheless, jumpy at the thought of trespassing. Mom had warned me about Quicksand Pond. She said cattle and horses were known to have been sucked in by the quicksand so deep no one could free them. I shivered. No doubt those skulls on the fence were from cattle and coyotes that had died that way, but seeing the size of the catfish skeletons hanging alongside them made me forget the danger.

What made this pond so good for fishing was that Winter-halter Creek fed into it, the clear water bringing with it the same big catfish that I have seen feeding on the bottom of the creek. Once the catfish find the slow-moving water of the pond they are content to stay there and scavenge on the mossy bottom, growing bigger and fatter by the minute.

My dad introduced me to the pleasures of reeling in a mon-ster cat—a fish large enough to make a meal to feed the whole family—and ever since I have been hooked. But as far as I knew neither my dad nor anyone else had ever fished Nurse Blanchett's pond. I don't think the old witch had ever let anybody cross her property line, much less help themselves to her pond.

As I baited my line, I remembered my mother's big smile, the kind reserved for her birthday and Christmas morning, every time dad brought home a stringer full of creek-bed catfish. I had a feel-ing I'd be seeing that smile real soon and any worries I had about what Nurse Blanchett might do to us if she caught us trespassing faded away.

While I had been daydreaming, Bo, Scotty, and Cecil had baited their hooks and begun casting their lines out over the sandy edge of the water. The water reflected the blue Oklahoma sky above and, as it lapped against the shore, it seemed to be saying, "Have I got a surprise for you!"

The four of us didn't talk much while we fished. We were too busy waiting for a catfish to pick up the scent of our worms. The sun warmed our backs. Horse flies buzzed about our faces. We brushed them away and waited some more.

Just when I was thinking I would never get a bite, I heard Bo cry out that he had one. I looked over as he pulled a nice-sized bluegill out of the water. It wasn't big enough to keep for us to eat, but it would make a mighty tasty meal for a catfish. Bo cut up the bluegill and shared pieces of it with us to use on our hooks.

Armed now with superior bait, I cast my line again and watched it sink under the surface of the water. It had barely disappeared when I felt a strong tug on my line. I thought I had hooked a mossy log, but then my line began moving and I knew I had snagged a big one.

I reeled it in slow to avoid breaking my line. I could tell this fish wasn't going to give up that juicy morsel of bluegill without a fight. A sudden hard tug on the line caused me to step forward, closer to the waterline. My foot sunk fast into quicksand. I tried to pull it out before the quicksand claimed my boot for good but lost my balance and stepped down hard with my other foot. Before I could yell for help, both legs were knee-deep in quicksand and sinking fast.

I should have been worried about saving myself, but the fish on my line demanded my attention. It was pulling so hard the tip of my pole had gone under water. I was close to losing it. Bo was closest to me, but he was a good ten feet away. Still he must have seen what was happening, because he hollered to the others to come help. He lunged for me and grabbed my shirt, working hard to keep me from sinking any deeper. Scotty came running with Cecil right behind him.

"Don't let her get away!" Scotty hollered.

I would have shot him a dirty look, but keeping my pole out of the water and my body out of the muck was taking all my concentration.

Bo latched onto me under my armpits and pulled with all his strength. The suction was so strong on my legs I thought they were going to come off—and if not them, then my boots. Bo rocked me back and forth, trying to work me free, while still pulling. Finally, the quicksand coughed, and I felt it release me. We both fell backwards, me on top of Bo.

It had been all I could do to hang onto my pole through the tussle with the quicksand. Now safely on dry land, I started reeling again, slow but steady.

"Here she comes!" Scotty yelled.

The fish broke the surface of the water and within seconds I had landed it. On shore she jumped and flipped and groaned. For a moment, I worried she was going to wriggle her way back into the pond before we could get our hands on her. I gathered my legs under me. They felt weak and rubbery, and I wasn't sure I could even run, but when Bo took off after my fish, so did I.

The fish jumped closer to the water as if she knew it was her only escape route. Bo and I dove for her at the same moment; Bo landed his knee on the fish's head and I landed my knee on her tail. We both knew the razor-like spikes on her dorsal and side fins were sharp enough to run us through, but without words exchanged we also both knew this fish wasn't going back into that pond.

Scotty rushed over with a stringer in one hand. He pushed the metal stake-end of the stringer through the fish's gill, slipped it through the ring on the other end to secure it, then pulled out the hook from the fish's mouth.

Bo and I stood and watched as Scotty raised the stringer with both hands till that fish was off the ground. Her head was at his shoulders and the tail almost dragged the shore. We stood gawking at the size, the fury, the beauty of one monster catfish.

My hands trembled. Thoughts popped through my mind, like popcorn in a hot skillet: *Mom is going to be so proud of me—I hooked a whopper of a catfish!*

"That cat must weigh a good twenty pounds!" I exclaimed.

"More than that," Scotty said. His arms looked like they were giving out as he lowered the catfish gently to the ground. "I bet it's closer to thirty."

Bo had to take a turn at guessing the weight. He picked up the stringer and lifted the fish with no trouble, but the look on his face said he was impressed.

"I bet it's the biggest cat ever caught in this county!" Bo said.

"I bet it's the biggest cat ever caught in the whole state of Ooo . . . klaaa . . . hoo . . . ma!" Scotty bellowed.

Cecil took the fish from Bo, holding the stringer with both hands and planting his feet shoulder wide for stability, while Scotty marched around them with his hands on his hips and a cocky grin on his face.

"She is a beaut," Cecil said. "We have to get her weighed."

"Tug's has an official scale," I said. Tug's is the only bait shop in town.

"How are we going to carry it all the way to Tug's?" Scotty asked. "That must be two . . . three miles."

"On a pole. Or a tree limb," Bo said. "We could tie the stringer onto it and then two of us could carry it between us. I've seen hunters haul deer like that."

The four of us searched for a tree limb worthy of the task. We spread out from the pond to do so. That's when Cecil spotted Nurse Blanchett's wood pile between the shed and another dilapidated outbuilding.

Scotty and I picked up the catfish and we all headed towards it. Her cats must have caught a whiff of the fresh fish, because before we knew it we were surrounded by a dozen meowing felines. They wanted a taste of our monster fish, but we weren't about to let them near it.

"Psssst!!" I hissed. "Get away! Go!"

Cecil and Bo tried to shoo them away, too. They ran right at the leaders of the pack, swinging their arms and hollering. The cats only retreated a few feet, then curiosity and hunger brought them right back to crowd us again.

Despite the feline distractions, Cecil managed to find a four-foot limb in the wood pile on which to carry the fish. He held the branch while Bo tied the stringer on it. Then Scotty and I each took an end of the limb and placed it on a shoulder. Bo and Cecil ran and grabbed our fishing gear, and the four of us got as far as the end of Nurse Blanchett's property before encountering our first obstacle: the barbed wire fence.

Chapter 6
Too Big to Handle

THE RUSTED BARBED WIRE fence loomed large as we stood before it trying to figure out exactly how to tackle our first big problem.

"You two could get on the other side," Scotty suggested to Bo and Cecil, "and we could pass her over."

"But the barbs are going to tear her skin." *No one was going to damage my record-size catfish.*

Before anyone could offer a better suggestion, the catfish grunted and swung its tail and nearly pulled the limb out my hands. Scotty and I did our best to hang on to the ends of the branch when I noticed Nurse Blanchett's cats circling us again. I gave them a nasty look and hollered for them to "git." The cats retreated a few feet, sat down, and began licking their paws as if they were cleaning up for supper.

Bo looked up and down the fence line.

"The only thing to do is follow this fence until we come to a place where we can cross."

"Guess so," I said. I was anxious to get moving anyhow. The cats outnumbered us and they were making me nervous. I didn't want nothing putting teeth marks in this beauty, except me.

Bo and Cecil led the way, carrying our fishing poles and tackle boxes, while Scotty and I followed, the limb stretched between us. I couldn't take my eyes off my catfish, hanging there between me and Scotty, swaying back and forth with each step we took.

A noise behind us made me turn and look, and I'll be a frog's uncle if those cats weren't still following us. They took my look as an invitation, and all of them—all twelve of them—came running up to us, meowing and cutting between our legs, tripping me and Scotty, rubbing their bony ribs against the fish's tail.

Scotty and I tried to run, but the heft of the fish and the motion of it swinging back and forth made it difficult. I was afraid the stringer might break any moment from the weight of the fish bouncing on it.

Meanwhile Bo and Cecil had set down all the fishing gear so they could concentrate on scaring away the cats. Despite their best efforts, those cats pestered us for near a half mile before they realized they were getting too far away from home and we had no intention of sharing what had to look like a feast-worthy catfish.

By the time they turned around, we had worked up quite a sweat trying to out pace them. And it seems things were going to get worse before they got better, too. At an old fork of Winterhalter Creek that I had never been to before, we ran into more trouble. We looked down into what was now a muddy ditch, overgrown with weeds, and it dawned on me that carrying this monster back to town was going to be much more difficult than I ever imagined.

The barbed wire fence crossed the ditch but didn't touch the creek bed at the bottom, leaving a gap wide enough for us to squeeze under it. The tricky part would be climbing down to the bottom of the ditch through the brambles and thistles, without harming the fish.

"This limb is cutting into my shoulder," Scotty said.

"I'll carry it," Cecil piped up.

Scotty handed over his end of the pole to Cecil.

"Looks like we can cross under," I said, sizing up the space between where the fence stopped and the creek began.

The others nodded in agreement.

"Why don't I go down first," Bo said, "and Scotty, you come down last, in case one of them two slips."

Bo turned around and backed his way over the edge, holding onto the tall weeds to keep from slipping. Cecil went next, holding onto the limb with one hand and weeds with the other. I held up my end of the pole high over my head to keep the catfish from dragging the ground. My arms began to shake as I edged over the side of the ditch, and then my boots began to slide on the slick grass. I was going down front ways so that I could guide the fish, but I was going too fast and about halfway down my feet slipped out from under me and I fell onto my bottom and slid down the creek bank right into the fish and Cecil. The three of us tumbled the rest of the way down and landed in thick mud at the bottom.

We were lucky we weren't gored to death by the limb or a fin. I took a minute to gather my wits before trying to stand up. The mud was slick, and when Cecil and I attempted to stand, our boots lost traction and we almost fell again.

"You two were a big help!" I yelled at Scotty and Bo.

Bo stood a few feet down stream. Scotty was still easing his way down the bank.

"They couldn't help it if you lost your footing!" Cecil yelled back. He was covered in mud from the waist down, just like me.

"Maybe we ought to call for help," Scotty suggested.

Cecil's face lit up. "Good thinking," he said, but his frown returned when he reached into his shirt pocket and tried to turn on his cell phone. "It's not working."

"Battery's dead," Scotty said.

"It's not much good to us then," Bo said.

"Darn thing," Cecil muttered. "What a waste of money."

Could things get any worse, I wondered.

My answer came soon enough.

While we'd been talking, the catfish had been flipping and flopping in the mud, coating herself with slippery wet red clay.

"Raise up your end!" I shouted at Cecil. "She's getting away!"

Cecil raised his end and I raised mine, but my arms were beyond tired. I didn't know how much longer I could hold up my end of the branch, and I had a feeling Cecil was wondering the same thing.

"How are we going to keep her from being scraped on them nasty looking barbs?" I asked, eyeballing the fence.

"I know," Bo said.

Bo pulled off the bright yellow T-shirt he was wearing.

"This should do it," he said, as he untied the stringer and slipped it through the neck of his shirt. Next he pulled the shirt down over the catfish. He pulled her side fins out through the armholes and tied the stringer back onto the limb.

"She looks like a scarecrow," Cecil said.

We all started to laugh. Cecil had broken the tension, and laughing together at that fish gave us a second wind.

"Let's just get out of here," I said. "You two are going to have to go under the fence first."

Bo and Scotty crouched and squeezed under the barbs of the fence. I then handed my end of the limb to Bo, and he pulled the fish through to where Cecil could hand over his end to Scotty. The fish and the shirt both made it through without a scratch or a tear. Now it was Cecil's and my turn. We got low and crawled under the fence. On the other side, I picked up my end of the limb, and Cecil picked up his, and we raised it to our shoulders.

The fish seemed heavier to me, but I wasn't going to give it up now. I had been in tougher situations. Seems keeping watch over a thirty-pound, three-year-old brother is good preparation for something like this, something that was important to me to finish.

We crossed the muddy ditch to where the bank wasn't as steep and climbed out. Then single file, we headed across a wide field of wildflowers and tallgrass teeming with butterflies under the late afternoon sun.

I could hear Winterhalter Creek before I could see it and I knew we were headed in the right direction. The only trouble was I had never been this far down the creek before and when we reached the row of trees lining it, the creek had grown into a river. Huge boulders jutted from the banks forming rocky cliffs that dropped ten feet to the churning, frothy water below. Winterhalter Creek must have been thirty feet wide here and who knew how deep.

"Can't cross here," Bo said.

"No duh," Cecil retorted.

"We'll have to follow it to a more shallow spot," Scotty said.

This time when Bo asked if he could carry my end of the limb, I was more than grateful to hand it over to him. My arms ached and my thighs burned. I was covered in sand from the pond, mud from the ditch, and burrs from the field. As I looked at each one of my buddies, I realized they were in the exact same condition. I had to respect them for not complaining about it.

The mud on the yellow shirt the catfish wore had dried into a brown crust. She didn't look much better than we did. But when she heard that water surging over rocks below us, she seemed to sense one last possibility of escape. With a grunt, she flipped her tail and smacked me in the face. I yelled out in surprise and rubbed my stinging cheek with one hand, while the other grabbed and held onto her for dear life.

The fear of losing our prize was enough to get us moving again. We took off, following the shady row of scrub oak that fed on the water of the galloping creek. We must have walked three-quarters of a mile, trudging through shoulder-high weeds, keeping one eye on the creek for a place we could either walk across—without having to climb down to it—or easily swim across.

We came to a slight bend in the creek where the water had

been slowed by a raised bed of rock, then dropped to form a waterfall, the only waterfall I had ever seen in these parts, waterfalls not being a common feature on the prairie.

"Looks like we could make it across here," Scotty said.

"Depends on how slippery those rocks are," Cecil said.

"And how fast that water's moving," I chimed in.

Bo adjusted the limb on his shoulder. "We best give it a shot, because it's getting late and my dad's going to be worrying."

With Bo's curfew nearing, we knew we had to go for it. We sidestepped down the slight incline to the edge of the water. Once again the catfish seemed to smell freedom, because she perked right up and began swinging her tail hard, hard enough to cause Bo to let loose of his end of the limb. Afraid we were losing her, I hollered, "Somebody grab it!"

Bo recovered fast enough to somehow catch his end of the branch before it could hit the ground and let the fish slip off.

"Here, let me do it," I said, more sharply than I meant to.

Bo didn't say a word, just handed his end to me.

I got a tight grip on it and gave a nod I was ready to go. Scotty went first, testing the stability of the rocks and the speed of the current with the toe of his boot.

"It's not bad." He put his full weight down. "Come on."

Cecil went next, holding tightly to his end of the limb. The catfish was doing her best to get free, flipping and flopping against the stringer. I don't know how she still had the energy at this point. I had to admire her fight. She must have been longing to feel that water, cool and murky, against her skin. Still we had caught her fair and square, and the thought of maybe losing her after all we had gone through to bring her home made me more resolved than ever to see this through. I grabbed the limb—holding her so tightly my knuckles turned white.

"Keep moving," I ordered, afraid that if we didn't hurry this fish would somehow get away from us for good.

Cecil glanced back at me, then ahead, and took a couple more

29

steps with me right behind him. Bo followed me as backup, so close I could hear him breathing hard. Then I heard what sounded like someone slapping his leg.

I looked around fast trying to figure out where the noise was coming from, when I saw the problem. The limb was breaking in two and there wasn't a thing I could do about it. I tried to grab for the stringer before it slipped off the branch, but my arms felt as if they were made of lead.

The catfish groaned with what could only be called delight as she fell out of my reach and into the water below. I could see her in that yellow shirt swimming closer and closer to the edge of the waterfall.

Cecil and I both dove for her, hitting the water hard on our bellies and then hitting the rocky bottom. The impact knocked the wind out of me, but it didn't matter. I had to reach her before it was too late. Cecil and I crawled and swam and grabbed for that fish, but she managed to always either be slightly out of our reach or to wiggle away.

I could hear Scotty's and Bo's panicked voices behind us, urging us on. Once I almost had her, but she darted away. Cecil got his hands on her only to have her again slip out of his grasp. I became a madman then, yelling and clawing at that fish. I splashed through the water on my knees, rose to my feet, and dove for her once more.

If it weren't for a scraggly branch hung up on a huge submerged rock, that catfish would be nothing but a fish tale that we told around campfires on starry nights. Instead, Bo's shirt snagged on the branch and kept that fish from sailing over the waterfall, never to be seen again.

Cecil and I reached her at the same instant, latched onto her with all our strength—my hands wrapped around where her body meets her tail fin, his arms around her neck—and brought her fighting to the opposite shore.

The stringer was still attached, so we plunged the stake into the ground and piled rocks on top of it to hold her there.

We both then fell onto our backs, breathing deep, satisfying breaths. My heart pounded in my ears as I lay there, exhausted.

Scotty and Bo came running over to us, smiling big smiles and laughing and slapping our legs. I raised up on my elbows, soaking wet, covered in green algae, and stared at that monster fish in awe.

"You're a fighter," I said. "No wonder you got so big."

The catfish grunted, defiantly.

"I thought she was gone for sure, this time," Cecil said.

"What we should have done was knock it out when we first pulled it out of the pond," Bo said. "I've seen my dad do that to catfish. Them other fish, bluegills, bass, and the like, don't last more than a couple minutes out the water, but catfish are different. They're hardy."

"Especially this one," I said.

"We're gonna need a new carrying stick, in any case," he said, looking around.

Scotty piled more big rocks on the stringer to ensure it stayed in the ground. The rest of us joined in until we were certain it was secure. Then we spread out in different directions along the shore to find another limb to use to carry her the rest of the way home.

The result was a pile of tree limbs in varying sizes.

I eyeballed the pile.

"So which one of us is going to do it?" I asked.

The guys seemed to realize I was no longer talking about picking a branch for the stringer.

My father had instilled in me a strong appreciation for the living things of the earth. I can still hear him telling me that you only kill what you are going to eat or use for something you need to live, and no more. So, I wasn't about to jump in and volunteer to put this fish out of its misery, even if I was planning to stock my mom's freezer with the meat. Yet somehow I also knew it would be far more cruel for the fish not to end it soon.

Nobody else seemed itching to do the deed, either, for instead of someone volunteering, they all looked at their feet or fidgeted with their hands in their pockets.

Finally, Cecil heaved a big sigh and said, "Okay, I'll do it."

We stood there, watching, as he chose the heaviest limb from the pile, raised it over the catfish, and brought it down hard on her head. The catfish didn't even flinch nor did it move again. I fought back tears, realizing in that instant that it is never easy to take a life, even when it's a dumb ol' fish.

No one spoke as Cecil picked up the stringer and tied it to the limb he had used for the clubbing. Bo and Scotty lifted the limb, balanced it between them, then raised it to their shoulders with one steady motion. They must have figured it was their turn to carry her, as both Cecil and I were spent.

The worst of the trip is now over, I thought, and that thought held true . . . for about five minutes. That's when we crested the bank of the creek and ran into what looked to be a jungle, only any settler from the 1800s could have told you was far worse: A patch of the Cross Timbers. In 1835, the author Washington Irving described crossing the Cross Timbers to be like "struggling through forests of cast iron." I shivered at the sight.

The Cross Timbers are an old dense strip of forest that slowed early American explorers traveling through Kansas, Oklahoma, and Texas to a crawl. It was far from ideal, but if we wanted to get back to Tug's before it closed—and get Bo home, too—we had no other choice. The forest becomes more dense with every prairie fire, and so it is matted with grapevines and green-briars that form thick, dense roughs. Explorers and settlers used machetes or sickles to get through the Cross Timbers in their day. We had only our bare hands.

Cecil moaned (we'd all had Oklahoma history in fourth grade, we knew a Cross Timber patch when we saw one), but to his credit, Cecil didn't hesitate, setting off through the dense thicket, chopping through the tangle of tree branches, vines, and briar with his arms and legs, slowly but surely clearing a path for us. I heard

32

what sounded like rabbits and squirrels scampering away. A doe and her fawns stood up suddenly, then bolted into the woods and out of sight.

Bo and Scotty, carrying the fish, followed Cecil.

I brought up the rear.

About ten yards in, Cecil pulled up and stopped, worn out from beating back nature. I eased past Bo and Scotty and the fish and took over for him. The thicket proved to be only about twenty yards wide, a blessing, really, given that it isn't unusual for the Cross Timbers to stretch for five to thirty miles in Oklahoma, but still it must have taken us half an hour to cross even those twenty yards.

When I broke through the last of the growth and out into the open, my face and arms were bloody from thorns and itching from burrs. I thought we were home free.

I was almost right.

A vast field of waist-high wheat lay ahead. If we had been walking in the direction of the wheat rows, it wouldn't have been a problem, we could have walked between them, but where we needed to go was straight across the field. That would have been tough enough going without toting along a catfish the size of ours, but with the stalks of wheat ready to blow their stacks, it was going to be near impossible for us to pass through.

Is it worth all this trouble? All I had to do was take one look at that record-size channel cat hanging on that stringer, so big and beautiful, dressed in Bo's tattered and creek-stained shirt, for me to know the answer.

Chapter 7
The Big Lie

TO OUR SURPRISE AND great relief, the main road ran along the other side of that wheat field. One look to our left, down that lonesome road, and our morale rose instantly, for there at the far bend sat Clem's Gas 'n' Go on the outskirts of Bootleg. A surge of energy lifted each step as we drew closer to town and Tug's Bait Shop.

I could only imagine the reaction from ol' Tug, who is prone to giving out more advice than a tree has leaves when it comes to fishing. Of course, Tug does know what he's talking about. Not once have I ever known him to give advice purely to sell a new, expensive lure or rod. If he had, in a small town like ours, word would spread as fast as spilt milk and before long all he would have to keep him company would be shelves full of fancy equipment.

Tug is a good businessman. Catch him when a new lure has just come in and you will see him handing them out to every man, woman, and child who comes into his shop. Samples, he calls them. If the lures work, he can't keep them in the store, be-

cause people buy them so fast—like I said, good news travels fast in Bootleg. If they don't work, he just quits selling them—'cause bad news travels even faster.

Lots of folks speculate on how Tug got his name. I think it came from him being such a good fisherman; every time he throws out his line he gets a tug on it. Cecil, now, he says Tug got his name because he is always tugging on something—his shirttail or his earlobe, his big nose, or his curly beard. But Bo told me that his dad told him that when Tug was being born he didn't want to leave his mama, and so the doctor literally had to tug on him to get him out. Been called "Tug" ever since. To this day Tug still lives with his mama. The name fits him, I think.

Once we reached the paved road, our gait picked up, and it took us no time to reach Clem's Gas 'n' Go. We decided to stop there first, since we were dying for a cold drink. As usual, Clem's was hopping with folks buying gas, chips, and pop. The very sight made my mouth water. It had been a long time since lunch.

I did begin to notice, however, that folks stopped dead in their tracks at the sight of us. I credited it to our unique looking scarecrow until I caught a look at myself in the reflection of the glass in the front door.

"Listen guys," I said, backing away from the door. "I think we ought'a clean ourselves up some. Us, and the fish."

Scotty eyed his reflection in the window and nodded.

"Yeah, if I didn't know it was me in that glass, I'd be scared."

I gave him a good once-over. "I am scared," I said.

"Restroom should be open," Scotty said, with a nod towards the side of the concrete-block building.

Cecil and I followed Bo and Scotty as they carried the catfish around to the side of the station, near the restrooms, and spread her out on the grass.

"We need to take her shirt off," Cecil said. "It's pretty ripped up. What do you say, Bo?"

"Go ahead," Bo said.

Having gotten the okay to tear Bo's shirt off the fish, instead of trying to take it off over her head, Cecil gave a pull on what was left of Bo's tee.

"It was an old one, anyway," Bo said, with a shrug.

None of us said anything, for we knew that most of Bo's shirts were old and came from the church rummage sale or the thrift shop. I don't remember the last time Bo had worn anything new-bought or that he particularly liked. But he had seemed partial to that yellow T-shirt, so it was generous of him to give it up for the sake of our mission.

While the catfish gleamed in the late afternoon sun, each of us took turns washing up. I was waiting for my turn, when Clem, the owner of the gas station, came around the corner from behind the building.

"What do we have here?" he asked, automatically taking measure of the weight and length of the catfish. "Did you catch that?"

"Yes sir, I did," I said, proud as anything.

"Wait until Ernie sees this!"

Clem went off in search of Ernie and by the time I had taken my turn in the bathroom and come out again, a crowd of four or five people had gathered around my fish. Bo and Scotty were posing with her for Ernie, so he could get a photograph of the unlikely trio.

"Here he is," Clem shouted over the oohs and ahhs coming from the circle of people, most of whom I knew. There was Greg Ganyon, who worked at the food store; Ray Burnes, from the bank; Andy Lowe, who goes to my church (he taught my Sunday school class last year); and some other guy who must have been passing through because I didn't recognize him.

"That's some catch," Ernie said, slapping me on the back and handing me a bottle of pop.

Ernie is Clem's younger brother. They look almost identical: tall and skinny, grease under their nails, toothpicks in their mouths no matter when their last meal had been. I had never seen either of them when they weren't wearing dirty red baseball caps with "Clem's Gas 'n' Go" in big black letters across the front.

I took a long swig of the pop.

"Yeah, well, we're taking it to be weighed at Tug's." I nodded to Cecil, Bo, and Scotty. "We'd best hurry. Bo's gotta get home soon."

"I'd like to see that fish get weighed," Clem said. "What do you think? Twenty-five pounds?"

"Close but I'd wager heavier," Ernie said. "You go ahead. I'll close up here."

"No. I think we'll just close up a few minutes early so we can both go."

"I bet that cat breaks all the records," Ernie said.

Before I knew it, Clem had turned off the gas pumps, locked up the store, and was following us, along with Ernie, to Tug's. I suppose Ray, Greg, Andy, and that other feller didn't want to miss out, so they came along, too.

The four of us Bulldoggers and my catfish were headed for Tug's, but we had to walk through the main part of town to get there. It felt like time was getting away from us again. I figured it was way past supper, late enough that the store owners in town would have closed up and gone home.

I was wrong. They were closing up, all right, but when they saw us coming with that catfish, every one of them stopped what they were doing so they could get a good look at my fish.

Unable to resist the excitement that goes with a possible re-cord-breaker, I guess, they all fell into line behind us. There was Joe Smythe from the hardware store; Miss Lucy and Mr. LeRoy from the café; Daniel Royce from the food store; Roger Chartel from the farmers co-op; and a whole bunch of kids on bicycles, skateboards, and scooters who tagged along for the heck of it.

To make matters worse, the catfish was taking on a bit of an odor, which drew a mess of cats. Bobby Frieze's Saint Bernard, Peaches, hates cats so you can imagine the chaos when Peaches suddenly decided to drag Bobby off the sidewalk to follow our clutter of feline fans. Peaches was on a leash and Bobby had been using her to tow him on his Rollerblades.

Things got crazy for a few minutes, what with the cats running amuck in the street and Peaches busting through the crowd, barking and slobbering after them, knocking people over and kids off their bikes. Nonetheless I felt I owed Peaches a word of thanks: the ruckus she caused kept the cats away from my prize fish long enough for us to reach Tug's.

By then, the crowd had grown too big for everyone to fit inside the little bait shop. Tug took one look at the fish, crossed himself like a priest, folded his hands together, and looked up to heaven.

"Holy Saint Francis, I can die now," he said.

I had never seen Tug cry before that.

"Somebody help the boys get that fish on the scale," he said, drying his eyes with a red bandanna. "Can't you see they're beat?"

Ray and Andy stepped up to help lift the catfish onto the scale.

"Wait, fellas. I think we could be talking an Oklahoma record. We have to get a state official here to witness this," Tug boomed.

He pulled his cell phone out of his pocket and dialed.

"Hello, Mark?" he said into the phone. "You best get yourself down here fast. I have a fish you're gonna want to see. Yep, I'm sure it's a record. Four kids brought her in. They're standing right here. Yeah, sure, and I'm eating supper with the president."

He paused, stood up a little straighter.

"Oh, well, excuse me. Sure, bring him with you. He's going to want to see this, too."

Tug turned off the phone, stuck it back into his shirt pocket, and gave us a big smile.

"Which one of you young fellas actually hooked this monster?" Tug asked, looking at each of us one by one.

I didn't hesitate: "That would be me."

"Congratulations, Dru. I think you might've broke some sort of state record with that channel cat. What'd you hook her on?"

"Bluegill," I said.

"And where on God's green earth did you catch her?"

My heart stopped. I could tell by how quiet everyone got that a lot of folks wanted to hear my answer. I looked at Bo. He looked down at his bare chest. I looked at Cecil. He leaned down to tie his shoelace. Scotty? He was fidgeting with his top shirt button.

"Well, son, where'd you hook her? I'm going to need to know for the form I have to fill out."

"Well, I . . . uh," I stuttered, trying to think of a plausible location fast. "I hooked her by the waterfall."

I heard chuckling rise up from the crowd.

"And what, pray tell, waterfall might that be? Niagara?"

More laughter from the crowd.

"No, sir. Winterhalter Creek, about two miles down from my house," I said.

"Laws, I'd nearly forgotten about that little creek, but you're right. There is a waterfall down there."

Joe Smythe piped up: "That's where old man Harlin's son drowned some fifty years ago."

"I bet no one has fished there since," Ray added.

A swell of voices rose up behind me as the group mulled this latest information over. I could hear disapproving murmurs behind me, as people realized the possible danger we had faced.

"Your parents let you fish there?" Tug asked, looking me hard in the eyes.

"Well, yes. Well, no. Well, they never did say one way or the other," I replied.

"Apparently, they should have. Sounds like there are some big channel cats hiding down in that little creek," Tug said.

Everyone laughed and the murmurs turned pleasant again, then a hush fell over the crowd.

"What's this big fish tale I'm hearing about?" a booming voice said from way in the back.

The man behind the voice made his way through the crowd, with another taller man following behind him. The shorter, gray-

40

haired man caught sight of the catfish hanging there first and his mouth dropped open.

"Dru, you might be the first one to ever render the governor of the Great State of Oklahoma speechless," Tug said.

The crowd chuckled and the murmurs turned to excited whispers as folks caught a glimpse of Governor Bill Ross.

"Governor," the taller man said, "this is Tug, the proprietor of this bait shop."

Tug shook hands with the governor.

"And who might we have here?" the governor asked Tug, motioning at the four of us with one of his large, hairy hands.

"Let's see now, Governor. This is Cecil, Bo, Scotty, and Dru," Tug said, pointing to each of us in turn.

"It's nice to meet you boys," the governor said.

He proceeded to shake hands with each of us. I was mighty glad we had made that restroom stop earlier and that I had used soap to wash up.

"Boys," Tug said, pointing to the taller man who had come in with the governor, "this here's the official we've been waiting for, Mark Stone. He's the State Fish and Wildlife Game Warden for Oklahoma."

We all shook hands with him one by one.

"This young feller here," Tug wrapped his arm around my shoulders as he spoke, "is the one who hooked her."

Mark Stone stepped up to the scale.

"I guess you're waiting to see how much she weighs?" He flashed a big, toothy grin at me.

I nodded.

"Fire this thing up, Tug," the game warden ordered.

Tug flipped on the switch. I thought those digital numbers would never stop changing.

"Thirty-six and a half pounds," Mr. Stone announced, finally. "We have a new Oklahoma channel catfish record!"

A cheer went up from the crowd.

"Well, son, it looks like you have made fishing history," said Mr. Stone.

I could feel myself beaming with pride.

I turned around to high-five my buddies.

They were nowhere to be seen.

Chapter 8
Proud as a Peacock

I COULD NOT FIGURE OUT where Cecil and Scotty could have gone. Bo, I knew, probably had bailed to get home on time to help his dad, but the other two, well, they had nowhere to be as far as I knew. And by disappearing like that they had missed having their pictures in the newspaper, with not only a record catfish but the governor himself.

While I waited for my dad to come pick up me and the catfish, I asked around about where my friends had gone. Everyone was still discussing the fish and its size and the record, badgering me about every little detail until I was plumb tired of smiling and talking.

But nobody seemed to have noticed when my friends left.

I knew my dad would have had to come in from the field and clean up before heading to town, 'cause it is his habit to come to town looking halfway decent, so I expected to have to wait a while for him to show up. But I never expected how excited he would be when he saw that catfish.

"Dru, my boy, looks like we have enough catfish here to feed not just the whole family but the whole town!"

His blue eyes were shining with pride and he was grinning from ear to ear. I grinned happily back at him and patted that fish like she was my best friend.

"Now where's that lucky rod you used to catch this monster?"

I frowned, realizing for the first time that I had left my fishing pole behind. "I . . . I lost it somewhere. Dang it."

Then I was brushed aside, as folks came up to shake hands with my dad, congratulating him on my breaking the record and telling him what a good job he had done teaching his boy to fish, saying they would be so proud if one of their sons ever brought home a fish that size. Meanwhile I was trying to retrace our steps from when we put the catfish on the stringer to when I last remembered seeing my fishing rod, but it was all a blur of mud and bugs.

"Dru," my dad said, smiling as big as Dallas at me. "You ready to go home?"

He was proud of me. I could feel it like warm sunshine on my back and by the way he carefully helped me carry the fish out to the pickup and spread her out nice and neat in the bed of the truck. He even offered me a piece of gum once we climbed into the cab and said he wished he had something more, but he couldn't think of nothing to top that prize fish.

By the time we pulled up to the house my mom had made a sign out of an old science fair poster I had made a couple years back and tacked it to the big oak tree by the driveway.

It read: "Congratulations on your record-breaker!"

Underneath the lettering, she had drawn a boy holding a fish as big as he was. She came running out the screen door of the house, camera hanging from one hand and Kevin bouncing on one hip—and she didn't stop running until she reached the pickup. She took one look in the bed of the truck and started to cry. I think they were happy tears.

She gave me a big hug and Kevin stuck his wet thumb in my

eye, by accident, but it was still nasty. I tried not to let it take away the goodness of the moment. After she was done hugging me, mom insisted on taking a picture for the family album.

"Dad, help him lift that fish out of there," she instructed.

My dad raised the fish up and out the bed of the truck, and handed her over to me. I had to hold the stringer with both hands to keep her from dragging her tail fin in the dirt.

"Steady now," Mom said, fiddling with the camera.

"Hurry, Blanche. The boy's arms are about to give out."

"One, two, three, say 'baloney,' " Mom said, and snapped the picture. "Let me take another one just for sure."

She took one more, just as my arms started to shake. Dad helped me carry the fish to the back porch where we cleared a spot to lay her down. Ma took another picture or two, then said, "I saved you some supper. Why don't you get cleaned up some while I warm it up for you?"

"What about the fish?" I said, afraid to leave it unguarded and worried that it might start going bad.

"He's right, Blanche. We better clean her now. She has been out of the water quite a while already."

"I'll get some newspapers," I said.

Dad went inside for his fillet knife. I spread newspapers out and filled a large bowl with water. Dad came back out and stood looking at the fish for a long moment, a funny look on his face.

"I think we might need the hacksaw," Dad said, shaking his head in amazement. "She's mighty big."

"I'll go get it," I said.

"You better bring the pliers, too," he added.

When I returned with the tools, Dad had me remove the fins. They were razor sharp, and no doubt I would have sliced myself to ribbons cleaning her if I hadn't done that first. Dad handled the next step, which was to cut off the head with the hacksaw. Her head was the size of mine and it took some effort to remove it.

"Do you want me to help you gut her?" Dad asked me.

"I think you best do it," I said.

"How about we both do it and we help each other? I'll do the cutting and cleaning, while you hold her steady."

"Okay," I said.

With the long, thin fillet knife, he slit open the belly of the fish like a skilled surgeon. Once he had cut out the intestines, stomach, and air bladder, he pulled off the skin with the pliers. Catfish don't have scales, which makes the job a little easier, but removing that skin is still no picnic.

My dad and I cut the meat into small pieces and tossed them in a bowl of salted water to soak. We cleaned up the mess we had made on the porch, then wrapped the fillets and stacked them in the freezer. By the time we finished up, I was so tired I couldn't see straight.

"Why don't you get cleaned up, son. I can get the rest."

"Thanks, Dad."

I went inside and smelled the remains of supper as I passed through the kitchen. Fried chicken was my guess. My stomach growled with hunger. I stopped in the bathroom. Mom was already filling the tub with water for my bath.

"I thought a hot bath might feel good to you tonight."

I nodded and yawned.

"Here are some clean clothes, too," she added. "Don't take too long or you might fall asleep from the looks of you."

She padded out on stocking feet, leaving me to undress.

As I peeled off my jeans and T-shirt, two questions pestered me: Was I ever going to get dinner tonight? And what had happened to Bo, Cecil, and Scotty?

I was counting on mom's promise to warm up dinner for me to take care of the first question. The second had me stumped. Why had my friends left so suddenly? Were they scared of someone finding out the truth about where we caught the fish? That was the only reason I could think of for why they had walked out on me in my moment of glory.

Chapter 9
The Morning After

DRU, GET UP . . . I MADE CINNAMON rolls for breakfast," Mom whispered in my ear, before padding out of my room. My mother had a way of making me want to get out of bed. As tired and stiff as I felt after yesterday, her cinnamon rolls were about the only thing in this world that could make me pry myself out of bed no matter how bad I felt.

Every muscle in my body screamed with pain as I rolled over and threw back the covers. It was all I could do to stand up. I stretched my arms over my head to loosen up my back muscles, then slowly bent over at the waist. As much as it hurt, it was the one sure way of working out the kinks, according to Scotty's dad, who should know, seeing as how he is a former rodeo champion.

I hunted around for a pair of jeans to slip into and I was snapping them at my waist when I heard mom say, as she passed by with Kevin toddling behind her, "Don't forget today is church!"

I looked over at the doorknob, and sure enough, as usual, there on a hanger hung my church clothes she had ironed for me.

I changed clothes again, still hurting all over, but beginning to loosen up some. I tucked in my shirt and wondered if I might run into any of the Bulldoggers at church today. Bo would more than likely be there, as would Scotty. Cecil was a different matter. Even though his grandma was a strict churchgoer, Cecil somehow managed to occasionally wiggle his way out of it. I wish I knew how he did it, because if there was ever a day I didn't feel like going anywhere, it was this one.

"Hurry up in there," Dad said, as he passed my bedroom doorway.

"Yes sir," I answered, as I sat on the bed to put on my shoes.

As I tied the laces, I thought about how Bo would be helping his dad get dressed for church about now, just in time for the parish van to pick them up and drop them off for the start of services. My dad had driven that van a few times when the regular driver was sick or gone and I had ridden along with him. At first, I saw the people who road the van as pitiful, too poor to even have a ride of their own to church, but then my dad told me how he admired them for being so dedicated to what they believe in that they would accept a ride to get there.

"Besides," I remember him saying, "it also gives us a chance to do something kindly for our neighbors."

I had never forgotten that.

I could smell mom's cinnamon rolls as I walked down the hall to the kitchen, and my stomach growled loudly in approval. I sat down at my place at the table and filled my plate with scrambled eggs, bacon, and two cinnamon rolls, for starters. I had just taken a big bite out of one of the rolls when my dad asked me a question that nearly made me choke.

"So, Dru. I never got to ask you last night, but just where did you hook that big ol' fish? At your usual fishing hole?"

I acted like I was still chewing. Dad had been skimming the Sunday paper, but when I didn't answer he put down the paper and looked at me, waiting for an answer.

48

"Uh no. It was farther down the creek."

That sounded more and more like the truth each time I said it.

"You'll have to show me the spot sometime."

"Okay," I said, and took a big bite of roll.

"Come on, now," Mom said, "or we'll be walking in during the reverend's sermon again."

I hurried to finish my breakfast. I was grateful my dad was too busy chasing Kevin around trying to put on his shoes to pay much attention to me.

I didn't need any more tough questions.

Chapter 10
The Lie Grows

THE TOWN OF BOOTLEG may be small, but like most towns and big cities in Oklahoma, there is a church on almost every corner. Given our town name, that probably surprises some folks. Given our history, I can assure you it would shock our town's founders.

But for the record, our town name is no play on the word bootlegger, which means somebody who makes or sells liquor illegally. Though from what I have overheard in town, it can still be difficult to get a drink on Sundays in Bootleg.

No, our town takes its name from good ol' Melbourne "Bootleg" Harlin. Harlin got his nickname after he lost a leg in a ranching accident and refused to give up wearing his cowboy boots. He had a fake leg attached to one, and he was known as Bootleg from that day on.

At one time Harlin owned most of the land around these parts, thousands and thousands of acres of prime grazing and farm land. Legend has it that most of his land holdings and spoils came from swindling the local Indian tribes, but as far as I know nothing was ever officially proven.

Until oil was discovered here, Harlin was one of the richest— if not *the* richest—men around here. The Harlin Ranch had its own newspaper, elevator, and telephone service (since no one else in town had a phone, Harlin used his to talk with people on the other side of his ranch). But Harlin's oversized ambitions for his Wild West Show did his empire in. That, and the Great Depression. Today the only reminder of that fancy mansion they called Harlin House is a crumbly brick foundation by the road.

My dad doesn't like to talk about what he calls "the Harlin days of Bootleg." He says that is all in the past, and this is the present. We can't change what was done before our time, no matter how shameful it makes us feel, but we can try to do what's right now and going forward and then maybe the future will be better.

I'm not sure I understand exactly what he means by that, but I do know what goes around comes around, and that's how come the Harlins have nothing left with their name on it here save for a little town no bigger than an oil spot.

As for the churches, well, they came later.

Our little church is no cathedral, but my mom says it's a friendly church that welcomes everybody. Having just caught a record-breaking catfish, I was a little more welcomed than usual this Sunday. Even the reverend couldn't resist a shout out to me from the pulpit.

After church I looked around for Scotty, Cecil, and Bo, but once again, they had disappeared.

Usually, while my mom and dad are busy talking with people after the service, the four of us would make plans for when and where we were going to practice roping.

With the upcoming rodeo only a week away, I had figured they would be wanting to practice every day after school. And since we had practiced at my house all last week, it was up in the air where we would be meeting this week. I chalked up their absence to their being as tired as I was after our big adventure, but still something didn't seem quite right. Something I couldn't put my finger on kept gnawing at me.

I didn't have much time to stew about it though, what with everyone coming up and congratulating me on my big catch. Seems there was a lot of interest in exactly where I had caught her, and each time I explained it to one or another of them it became clearer in my mind.

When Clayton Hilsinger, a kid in my class at school, asked me about it, I told him, "Down at the waterfall on Winterhalter Creek."

But when Alan Thomas, another kid at school, came up to me, busting to know where I had caught her, I told him, "Down off the big rock jutting out by the waterfall."

And when Mr. Schwarz, a friend of my dad's, asked me, I told him, "You know that craggy place where all the trees are caught up? It was in there, I think."

By the time we got home from church, I wasn't feeling so good. Besides my other aches and pains, my stomach now hurt, too. I told my mom I was going to lay down for a while only to have her give me one of her worried looks.

"I'm just tired," I said, quietly. "Yesterday was a long day. It's a lot of work hauling in a thirty-six-pound catfish and carrying it to town."

I risked a glance at her to see if she would take the bait, while at the same time hoping she wouldn't get it in her head to cover me with stinky ointments or bother me with thermometers and hot water bottles. My mom believes wholeheartedly in that dumb ol' saying, an ounce of prevention is worth a pound of cure, only she thinks it means a pound of cure is the prevention part.

She must have found my reasoning reasonable, because she let me go to my room without any more questions. She just headed to the kitchen to start Sunday dinner.

After supper, I tried calling Scotty, but his mother said he didn't want to talk to me just then. I tried calling Cecil next, but I got the answering machine, and when I called Bo, his dad said he was out tending the stock.

I went outside and threw a few loops over the roping dummy my dad had set up for me in the shade of the pecan tree, but my heart wasn't in it.

When Mom called me in to get ready for bed because it was a school night, I thought about telling her I wasn't feeling so well and maybe I should stay home from school tomorrow, but then I realized she would surely call the doctor this time—or worse start dispensing one of her homemade remedies. The thought of being poked and prodded by Doctor Haznott didn't sound fun.

But it was the thought of my mom's homemade concoctions that changed my mind. *Surely, facing school couldn't be as bad as one of her remedies*, I thought.

Deep down, I wasn't so sure.

Chapter 11
Let's Make a Deal

I ALMOST MISSED THE school bus Monday morning. I got my chores done on time: Fed the chickens and horses, collected eggs from the hen house. But when I went to get dressed for school I couldn't find my boots and once I found them, they were covered with dirt. Then I couldn't find my science book. Come to find out, Kevin had carried it off to his room and hid it under his bed, for what reason I couldn't tell you. Who knows the thoughts that go through that baby brain of his.

When I finally managed to get out the screen door, I could see the bus was ready to pull away from my stop and if I hadn't run as fast as I could and banged on the door, the bus driver would have left me behind in her dust.

I climbed aboard and found a seat, midway back, by an open window. The seat was kind of sticky, and the air coming in from outside felt, thick and heavy. I looked out and saw gray thunder clouds in the sky. Maybe it was going to rain. That must be it. Rain. Most times the sky in Oklahoma is clear, blue as blue can be, and sunny. I hadn't seen rain for a long time. Not since Good Friday.

My mom says it always rains on Good Friday, but mostly what I remember from the last one was puddle jumping in the driveway with Kevin. The puddles came up to his knees, but he didn't seem to care. And his attitude was contagious. Running from puddle to puddle, we jumped and splashed in that muddy water until we were soaking wet and sporting globs of mud from the tops of our heads to the tips of our toes.

The sound of someone calling my name brought me back to the present. I turned around to see who it was and saw Cash Bennett coming up the aisle of the bus. He plopped down on the seat next to me.

"Hey, Cash. What's up?"

"I heard about that channel cat you caught. Way to go."

He high-fived me.

"Thanks," I said, with a grin.

"Where'd you hook a monster like that? Thirty-some pounds, I heard."

"Thirty-six and a half."

"Right," he said.

Cash fiddled with the strap on the backpack he was holding before looking at me straight in the eye.

"Well, anyway, where was it?"

"Why do you want to know?"

Cash was one of those kids who is always asking questions, and not the kind of questions people like to answer. He was more like a gossipy girl, nosing into other people's business. Habit made me give him a hard time about it.

"Like I said, 'Why do you want to know?' "

"Just curious," he said, almost apologetically.

"You're never just curious about nothing."

"Some people are wanting to know is all," he said, pushing his glasses up on his nose with his thumb.

"It's no secret," I said, frowning, "but what exactly do you mean by 'some people'?"

"You know, some guys at school."

"You mean, you want to know where I caught it so you can go try to break my record."

Cash sat up a little straighter, looking a mite defensive.

"What if I do?"

"Okay, already," I said. "You know where that waterfall on Winterhalter Creek is?"

"Yeah, I've seen it. That's where you hooked it?"

"Yup."

"Was it above the waterfall, or below?"

"Above," I said.

The bus turned into the circle driveway in front of the school and stopped. I stood up, signaling to Cash that our conversation was over. He didn't take the hint.

"Where *exactly* did you hook her?" he asked, frowning, not budging from his seat.

"It was in the brush caught up under a big flat rock that juts out from the bank. Is that clear enough? Everyone's getting off the bus. I have to get to class."

Cash gave me a puzzled look, stood, and followed me, as we filed off the bus, the last ones to leave.

I headed for the hickory tree in front of the school. It was the meeting place for us Bulldoggers before school. I spotted Bo and Cecil with their heads together deep in conversation behind the old tree.

"Hi guys," I called out as I approached them. "What are you doing?"

No response.

"Where's Scotty?" I glanced around at the kids milling about the school parking lot or gathered in small groups on the front lawn of the school.

Just then, Scotty broke through the crowd and came walking

towards me. He did not look happy to see me.

"Dru, we need to talk," he said in a strangely deeper than normal tone of voice.

Before he could tell me what it was we needed to talk about, Bart the Buffoon and Weasel Jack sauntered over to us—never a good thing.

"We have a proposition for you," Jack said.

"Yeah, a *preposition*," Bart repeated.

"No, you fool, not a *preposition*, that's some sort of English term," Jack said, scowling. "We have a proposition. A deal."

"Yeah, a deal." Bart nodded and smiled a crooked smile.

"What's this all about?" Cecil asked.

"I'll tell you what it's about," Jack said, lowering his voice. "It's about that fish you guys hauled out of that ol' witch's pond."

"How'd you know about that?" I asked.

"Never you mind. We have our sources," Jack said. "Anyway, here's the deal. You guys do a few favors for us and nobody will ever know where you caught that fish. Otherwise, we're going straight to Tug's."

"What kind of favors?" Scotty asked.

"You'll find out in due time. Do we have a deal?"

"Do we have a choice?" Cecil asked, sarcastically.

"Sure, if you want everybody to know where you really caught that fish."

The four of us shook our heads.

"We'll meet you here after school for your first assignment."

"More like misdeed," Scotty said.

"Whatever," Jack said.

He and Bart took off.

The homeroom bell rang before we could say anything more.

Chapter 12
The Missed Deed

THE FOUR OF US HURRIED into the school and ran to the sixth-grade classroom. Mrs. Wheely was taking roll as we slid into our seats. I glanced over at Scotty, but he refused to catch my eye. Mrs. Wheely told us to take out our math books. I had a hard time concentrating on math and every other subject that morning, worrying about what sort of things those two helmet-heads would make us do.

At lunchtime, I thought I would have a chance to talk to Bo, Cecil, and Scotty, but some girls kept hanging around and we were all afraid to say anything about you-know-what.

By the time we met up by the hickory tree after school my nerves were strung so tight you could have played "Yankee Doodle" on them. Gray clouds had threatened rain all day, but now I could see lightning off in the distance. At first, I thought it might have been the static in the air plucking my nerves, but deep down I knew better.

Jack and Bart were waiting for us at the tree.

"About time," Jack said, scowling at me.

I started to snap something back, but Jack hushed me before I could get the words out.

"I don't want to hear none of your pre-school gibberish, you hear? I know you guys aren't the brightest bulbs in the box so I will make it simple."

He strutted back and forth before us like he was some sort of drill sergeant sizing up a line of new army recruits.

"When Ashley comes to work at the drive-in this afternoon, we want you to let the air out of her tires."

"Oh, I get it," Bart said. "Then she'll need a ride home."

"Shut up!" Jack barked at Bart.

He turned his attention back to us.

"She comes to work at four o'clock," he told us. "She drives a white Honda. I have to go to work, but I'll be watching, so don't mess this up, or else. Come on, Bart."

As they strode away, Jack punched Bart in the arm. It looked like he was giving his not-so-bright buddy a good talking-to.

Once they were out of earshot, Bo turned to the rest of us with a look of relief on his face.

"That's not as bad as I had imagined."

"Yeah, it could've been worse," I said.

"No. Missing my bus is worse," Scotty said, "and there it goes."

We turned around in time to see our buses pulling away from the school.

"We'll just have to find another way home," I said. "After we let the air out of Ashley's tires, that is."

"You have all the great ideas, don't you?" Scotty said. "Now look at the mess we're in. When are we going to practice? I have a lot riding on this roping."

"We all do," Cecil said, "but we're also all in this together."

"Not if you listen to Dru tell it. According to him, he's the one who caught the fish all by himself at the waterfall," Scotty said. He angrily gave the tree a swift kick. "If I don't score well in this competition my dad said I might as well give up trying to make a go at rodeoing."

"Yeah, right," Cecil said. "He never said no such thing to you. You're making that up, because you don't want to help out."

"Are you saying I'm lazy?" Scotty's face was red.

"If the boot fits," Cecil said.

Scotty balled his hands into fists.

Bo stepped between them.

"See what those two clowns have done to us already? They have us bickering like Bantam roosters."

"If it weren't for Dru and his big mouth," Scotty said.

"Would you rather I had told them about Quicksand Pond?" I asked. "Would you? Do you want Witch Blanchett to know that we were on her property?"

"I'm not talking about where the fish was caught. You took all the credit. You should pay the price," Scotty said.

"Hold on guys," Bo said. "Dru was just excited at Tug's, and besides he is the one who hooked her in the first place. Let's just go take care of business, and then we can go practice over at my place. Dad said it would be all right."

"Bo's right," Cecil said. "We would be up a creek if anyone finds out where we caught that fish. What's it going to hurt to let a little air out of a tire or two? Then we can get to what's important. Practicing."

"I guess you're right," Scotty said. "But, if I know them two, this is just the beginning of the favors. They're testing us to see if we'll do what they say."

"A few favors is what they said," I said. "Then it'll be over. They'll forget about us and we'll be off the hook."

"Yeah, we won't be worth their trouble after that," Bo said. "And if it turns out that Ashley takes a liking to Jack, he'll be too busy looking at her to bother with us."

"It's already three-thirty," I said. "By the time we walk over to the drive-in, it'll be about four."

"Maybe Clem has something we can borrow to use on the tires," Cecil said.

We hiked over to Clem's Gas 'n Go and found Clem sweeping the sidewalk. I explained that I needed to borrow a pin because my bike tire was flat.

"You don't need a pin for that," Clem said.

"Did I say bike? I meant to say basketball," I lied.

"That's different," he said. "Anything for the best fisherman in town."

I felt only a little twinge of guilt about lying to Clem, but I reckoned my story was half true. My bike tire and my basketball were both flat . . . at home.

We got to the drive-in a few minutes before four o'clock. The sky was clouding up and I heard thunder in the distance. Ashley's white Honda was already in the parking lot.

"We'll stand here and pretend we're talking," Scotty said to me, "while you let out the air."

I ducked down behind the others, and we inched our way over to Ashley's white Honda. It was parked beside Jack's black dually; with its extra set of wheels on the back, you couldn't mistake his truck. His pickup hid her car from view, pretty much.

I worked fast and within minutes, all four tires were flat.

Thunder crashed overhead as I finished up.

I stood up just in time to see a little white Honda squeal into the parking lot with Ashley at the wheel. She parked her car and dashed inside the restaurant at the stroke of four.

Chapter 13
Tipping Cows

IT TOOK ONLY AN INSTANT for what we had done to sink in and the trouble we were going to be in to register on our faces. Scotty, Cecil, and Bo seemed dumbstruck. I managed to croak out a question.

"Now what?" I asked.

It was all I could get out. None of our options seemed good. Scotty made the call.

"We have no choice. Do we?"

"But her car is parked right out in the open," Cecil said.

"Let's wait a few minutes," I said, "and see if anyone parks beside her. If we only let the air out on one side, she'll still need a ride home."

We waited, and sure enough another car pulled in next to hers.

"Let's go," I said.

Once more, we set to work. The other three covered me while I did the deed.

"Done," I said, finally. "Now let's get out of here."

We lit off down the street like we were Olympians in the hundred-yard dash. The adrenalin was pumping so hard I thought we might be able to even outrun the storm, but I was wrong. We made it to the bend in the road outside of town when the sky cracked open and poured rain down on us.

There was no shelter in sight. That's when I remembered the abandoned storm cellar, the one we used to use as a hideout when we were ten and playing outlaws.

"Go left," I yelled to Scotty, who was a few feet in front of me.

I could barely make him out in the downpour. I made a sharp left into the thick grass by the road. Bo and Cecil followed.

If I remembered right, the storm cellar was only a few feet ahead of me. I bent down and began feeling around in the underbrush for the door handle. When I found it, I tugged on the heavy metal door with everything I had until it popped open. The four of us slipped inside just before the storm kicked it up a notch.

I hadn't been down in that cellar in a long time and who knew what kind of critters might have made their homes there since my last visit. My mind ran down a nasty list: poisonous fiddleback spiders, deadly copperheads, furry tarantulas, red-hourglass-bellied black widow spiders, scorpions. I shivered. Maybe we had traded the storm for something worse.

My feet were getting wet. Water had leaked inside, too.

Above us, we heard what sounded like the roar of a train running over the top of the shelter; maybe, we had escaped a tornado. Or maybe it was just high winds. It can be hard to tell when you are in the middle of either. The rain pounded the metal door. Not one of us made a noise. Or moved. We were too scared. We may have been in shock, too, because I didn't squirm even when it felt like something was crawling up my back. It felt like we waited hours for that storm to pass. Finally, the pounding and the rain stopped.

"Do you think it's gone?" Scotty whispered.

"I don't hear anything," I said. "I'll take a look."

But when I tried to raise the storm door, it wouldn't budge. I heaved and hawed. I lifted with my back. I pushed with both hands. "It's stuck!"

Bo, Cecil, and Scotty squeezed in around me and put their hands on the cellar door, ready to push.

"On the count of three. One . . . two . . . three!"

We lifted with all our strength.

The cellar door flew open and slammed the ground with a loud wet thud. Scotty scrambled out first to take a look around.

"The coast is clear," he said.

Bo climbed out next, and then Cecil. I was the last one out.

"You know, this cellar would make a cool clubhouse if we were to fix it up some," I said, as I worked the kinks out of my back.

"Nobody would ever find us in there," Cecil said.

"That's what I was thinking, too," I said.

"I don't know about that," Cecil said, "but if I am late getting home one more time my grandma said she would horsewhip me."

"Your grandma wouldn't horsewhip nobody," Bo said. "I have seen her carry spiders outside and let them go."

"No matter," Cecil said. "I don't want to have to spend all Saturday making up for being late tonight."

Everyone groaned in agreement. We all knew from experience that being late could mean extra chores that would eat up all of our Saturday, which would mean no chance of going to the rodeo.

. . . .

The next morning we met up on the breezeway of the school. It had rained on and off all night, and I was hopeful the rains would keep Jack and Bart from finding us. No such luck. Jack and Bart splashed their way across the swamp of a lawn to us.

"Here they come," Cecil said, "and none too happy, neither."

I had fallen asleep to the pelting rain on our roof at home. Now I wished I had stayed under my covers, tucked safely away

65

from the two angry jerks who were fast approaching.

"Nice job, you morons," Jack said.

"Yeah, nice job," Bart echoed.

"If it wasn't for you numbskulls messing up I could have been making time with Ashley," Jack ranted. "Instead I ended up driving home that moronic manager in the storm and listening to him whine about vandals. I should have squealed on you guys right then, but I have a better idea. I'm going to teach you a lesson you won't forget."

"Yeah, if Ashley's boyfriend hadn't been there at closing . . ."

"Shut up, Bart!" Jack bellowed.

"The rest of this week Bart and I are supposed to do what they call 'community service,' but I am going to help you help us. I am going to let you do it for us."

"What kind of community service?" Cecil asked.

"You'll find out soon enough. Just meet us behind the city office building at a quarter to four. And if you don't show, well, you know what'll happen."

Jack pulled his thumb across his neck in a slicing motion.

Enough said.

"But . . ." I sputtered.

"No fat butts about it. Be there," Jack ordered.

After Jack and Bart took off, Scotty turned to the group.

"Sounds to me like Jack's mad, because he didn't know Ashley had a boyfriend," Scotty said.

"Yeah, and now we have to pay for that, too," Cecil said.

"But it's nice of them to do community service," Bo said.

"Naw, that's what they make you do when you've broken the law," I explained.

"I heard they were caught trying to tip cows in Mr. Wainright's field," Scotty said.

"Yeah," said Cecil. "Their plan was to sneak up on his herd in the middle of the night, while the cows were sleeping, push a couple over, and run like their pants were on fire."

"But cows don't sleep standing up," Bo said, "and anyway, how could two guys push over a half ton of cow?"

"I didn't say tipping cows was doable," Cecil said, "but numb-skulls like Jack and Bart wouldn't know that."

"Seems Mr. Wainright," Scotty said, "fired a shot at them for trespassing. Jack and Bart were in such a hurry to get out of there that they ran over a barbed wire fence in Jack's truck. The barbs flattened the tires, and the sheriff didn't have any trouble catching up with them."

We almost missed the homeroom bell for laughing so hard.

Chapter 14
Picking Up Trash

B Y THURSDAY WE WERE SO sick and tired of picking up trash people had thrown out of their cars along the highway, I swear I was doing it in my sleep. I have never been able to understand why it is so difficult for some people to hold their trash until they come to a trash can. There is always a trash can someplace: rest stops, Sonics, gas stations. And if they can't find a trash can, why couldn't they just throw it away once they got home like normal people do?

Geez, I'm starting to sound like my dad.

Being from the land, he holds a natural respect for it and I guess it has rubbed off on me. I may not enjoy picking up trash, but I can see why it needs to be done. Litter takes away from the natural beauty of our community—and that's something we can all enjoy no matter whether we're rich or poor or just driving through.

Yeah, Jack and Bart's community service was picking up litter along the roads in and out of Bootleg. We were still not happy about serving their time, just because we let the air out of the wrong tires. But at least we were doing something useful instead of sneaky. At least that's the way I tried to look at it.

We picked up trash for two hours each day and if that doesn't work your back into a knot, nothing will. Then, on top of that, we had been meeting at Bo's to practice our throwing techniques; that is, when it wasn't raining. Rain may be good for growing wheat and watermelons, but it's hard on a boy's throwing skills.

It had gotten to the point that by the time I got around to doing homework I was about beat to pulp. I could barely keep my eyes open. But the rule at my house is if I don't keep up with my homework, then I have to give up rodeoing, and you know how I would feel about that.

So there I was sitting at the kitchen table trying to read a chapter in my science book, rubbing my eyes to clear them enough to read the text, when my dad came in for a drink of water.

"Pushing yourself mighty hard these days, Dru," he said, as he took a glass from the cabinet and ran water from the faucet.

"Yeah, well, I guess," I said, and yawned.

"What have you been doing? I haven't seen much of you this week."

"Practicing for this weekend, mostly," I said, crossing my fingers behind my back.

"Ernie said he thought he saw you out along the highway. He said it looked like you were picking up trash."

"Oh," I said, trying to think of some story he might believe. "School project."

"Sounds like a good idea, but don't overdo it, or you'll just be cutting off your nose to spite your face, if you know what I mean."

Boy, did I know what he meant. It seemed like I was cutting off my whole face lately, not just my nose. How did I get in this mess? The guys were still acting kind of mad at me, and the trash deal had made things worse. We weren't getting much time to practice, and besides that, I had heard tell that people had been fishing that spot above the waterfall so much there was a traffic jam along the roadway, trucks and cars parked every which way. (If only we had known the road came so close there we would never have had to walk through that jungle of Cross Timbers or through that wheat field, both of which nearly kilt us.)

"Well, Dad, I was meaning to ask you if you, well, I mean, was there ever a time when you found yourself in a mess you didn't know how to get yourself out of?"

"Well, son, sure. There've been plenty of times like that, but you know what they say: the best way out is always through. I think it was Robert Frost who said that. You know, the poet."

He looked me in the eye.

"Is there something you want to tell me, son?"

I shook my head.

What he said made sense, but "going through" this mess would mean having to explain that I had lied to him and everyone else in town. I didn't know if I could do that.

He patted my shoulder as he left the kitchen and headed to bed.

"You'll figure it out. You're a smart boy."

The best way out is always through, I repeated to myself.

I found my place on the page of my science book and kept on reading.

Chapter 15
Picking Trash, Again

WHEN THE SCHOOL BELL rang Friday afternoon, I could hardly wait to get home. All week long I had been so busy doing "community service" and homework and chores that I had hardly thrown a half dozen loops. Saturday, tomorrow, was the roping competition. I had barely had time to get Checkers worked into shape, but come rain or come snow, I was going to have to get a'horseback. The judges don't take no excuses, they just count you as you come, and if you don't measure up, you're out.

My stomach flip-flopped when I saw Jack and Bart waiting for me after school. Cecil, Bo, and Scotty were already corralled and scowling. They were probably thinking like me, *here we go again*, picking trash till we're blue in the face, when we should be roping.

"Took you long enough," Jack said to me, then he turned to face Bo, Cecil, and Scotty.

While his back was turned and Bart was eyeing some high school girls walking past, I made funny faces at Jack and Bart. I wiggled my ears, puffed out my cheeks, and crossed my eyes. Bo, Cecil, and Scotty tried not to laugh, but I could tell they wanted to.

"Don't you guys forget to show up today," Jack ordered, "or you'll be sorry."

"I thought we were done with that deal," Bo said.

"Yeah, me too," Cecil blurted out.

"The roping's tomorrow," I said. "We've done your grunt work all week, and between that and the rain, we've hardly worked a rope in days."

"Poor babies," Jack said in a syrupy tone of voice. "Ain't that just too tough. I guess we'll just have to stop by Tug's on the way home, Bart. What do you say?"

Bart was still distracted by the girls.

"Tug's? Oh, right, Tug's." Bart nodded with vigor. "Yeah, he'd sure be interested in what we have to say for once."

"Yup, mighty interested," Jack said.

"Okay, okay," I said, thinking my dad would be none too pleased to find out I had lied to him. He would probably ground me and I wouldn't get to compete at all. "We'll do it."

Bo, Cecil, and Scotty must have had similar thoughts, 'cause they were nodding, too, but with little enthusiasm, that's for sure. Jack and Bart strode off then, laughing and slapping each other on the backs, like they were swatting flies.

"Them two boneheads have us cornered," I said, once they were out of earshot. "If they tell Tug, my dad sure as shooting won't let me out of the house tomorrow."

"That's what I was thinking, too," Bo said.

"Who are the boneheads now?" Scotty asked, sarcastically.

"I'd say it was us," Cecil answered. "We're the ones doing their dirty work."

"As I said before," I said, "it could be worse."

"I don't want to think about it being any worse," Cecil said.

"Me, neither," Bo chimed in. "Let's just get it over with so the whole day isn't used up before we get to practicing."

The Bulldoggers Club

We all knew that the bit of pocket money Bo might win from roping meant all the difference for him and his dad when it came to being able to buy stuff they needed.

Decision made, the four of us trash-pickers loped off towards the city offices. There we were handed big black trash sacks and plastic gloves and assigned which spot we would be scouring for cigarette butts and Styrofoam cups, beer cans and plastic pop bottles today.

One thing was for certain: we would have plenty of time to think about what we were missing.

Chapter 16
Getting a'Horseback

SATURDAY MORNING DAWNED clear and bright. A cool easterly breeze at my back egged me on as I ran laps around the cow pasture. I had been up before the sun came up and had slipped on my jeans and sneakers and tiptoed out the screen door at first light, before anyone else was out of bed. Running laps limbers me up for roping and helps keep my legs strong and my breathing even when competing. I am ashamed to say I haven't been running as much as I should have, and not nearly as much as Scotty's dad said we should do.

I could hear coyotes howling off west a good ways out, howling at what was left of the moon, I figured. Once the sun came up those same coyotes would go cowering into the shadows for a snooze in the wet grass.

As for me, my favorite time of day is in the still of the morning, when everything looks fresh and new, the way it must have looked on the world's very first day.

Last night when I got home, I skipped supper and went

to the barn to shine the leather on my saddle, bridle and roping reins, as well as the boots that protect Checkers's legs when he is keeping with a darting calf, stopping and starting and turning fast. I brushed out the mud caked in his mane and tail. He was a sorry sight after wandering through the pasture in search of sweet grass.

I couldn't wait to get a'horseback and limber Checkers up for the day's runs. As a rule, I ride him for an hour or two every day the weeks before a rodeo, but this past week I had been lucky to ride him at all. It was going to make it tougher on both of us, because, if nothing else, a horse and his rider need to be able to read each other's mind when it comes to roping calves. And that takes putting the hours in so horse and rider work as one.

Having cut our training short, I now had to rely on the knowledge that a good cow horse usually knows more about roping cattle than his rider. My dad might be the one exception to that rule. He knows more about roping than just about anybody. He broke Checkers to the saddle, and he let me help so I would learn how to break a colt, for future use. Checkers has been on every roundup I can remember, both at our ranch and at the neighbors'. Around here everybody helps everybody else when it comes to spring and fall roundups, and at harvest time, for that matter.

Laps finished, I headed inside to change into my roping clothes: boots, jeans, and a long-sleeved shirt. When I went to put on my belt, my lucky belt buckle came up missing. My Uncle Dave had brought it back from his trip to Mexico last year. I was sure I had put it in my top dresser drawer, but it wasn't there now.

I grabbed a handful of buttermilk biscuits off the counter, snatched my Stetson off the coat hook on the back porch, and took off for the barn. Checkers was looking for me, his head hanging over the stall gate, just as anxious as I was to get moving. I saddled him and led him out of the stall and through the barn to the corral, where I started taking him through the practice course, just like my dad had taught me.

Round and round we went, first one way, then the other, all at a good lope with me riding the stirrups, which means standing in them, until we were going at a good speed. I could tell Checkers was tight and jumpy the first few go-rounds, but it didn't take long for us to work into our usual smooth rhythm, and I could feel my confidence coming back. No longer was I feeling edgy and nervous, instead I was excited and anxious to make my runs.

I looked up to see Dad hooking up the horse trailer to the pickup and knew he would be ready to load Checkers soon. I took Checkers for a few more practice runs across the arena before we quit for good. Practice over, I made sure to walk Checkers to cool him down before giving him a helping of oats—not too much for fear of overfilling his stomach—to fuel him for our big event.

Now it was time to feed the rider. I opened the screen door to the kitchen just in time to see mom frying eggs the way I like them, sunny-side up with plenty of runny yolk for dipping.

"Wash up, Dru. I'll have your plate ready in a jiffy."

I washed up in the kitchen sink, dried off on the tea towel, poured myself a big glass of milk, and sat down at my place at the kitchen table.

"So, you think you and Checkers are ready?"

"He rode pretty good," I said.

"I'm sure you'll do just fine," she said, and set my plate down in front of me. She had filled it with eggs and hashbrowns, biscuits and sausage gravy.

I took a big bite of biscuits and gravy.

"I oh I ooo etter an ine," I mumbled.

"Don't talk with your mouth full, Dru. How many times do I have to tell you that? Now, what did you say?"

I swallowed. "I said, I hope I do better than fine."

"Just do your best. That's what we expect of you. Your best."

Her words made me think about how I had failed to do my best in so many ways the past week, the least of which was not practicing enough. Did I even deserve to do well at the roping today?

Before I could say anything else, Kevin toddled into the kitchen, trailing a laundry sack behind him that bumped and rattled across the kitchen floor.

"What have you got there, bud?" I asked.

"Teshur," he said.

"Treasure?" I repeated.

"Yesh."

"Can I see?"

Kevin's eyes lit up, and he began to pull stuff from his bag, one thing at a time. First, a lid from a pot, then a chewed-up toy truck, my mom's silver hair barrette, and finally my brass belt buckle!

"How'd you get a hold of that?" I asked, grabbing it away from him.

Kevin's face clouded over, and he began to wail a baby wail that spun Mom around from the stove, spatula waving. She could immediately see what had happened.

"Why did you do that?" she yelled over the teary siren blaring at her feet.

"Do what? It's mine!" I yelled back.

"You should've put it away."

Kevin took a breath, building up for another ear-piercing scream. I filled the vacuum as fast as I could.

"I did, but he gets into everything, no matter where I put it."

The scream filled the room. Mom grimaced.

"You'll just have to be more creative at hiding things."

"You always take his side," I yelled back.

"He's only three years old!"

"So?"

With that she picked Kevin up and began to rock him back and forth. "Dru, finish your breakfast."

That was my mom's way of ending a discussion. I put on my lucky belt buckle and did what she had told me to do: I stuffed my face.

My lucky belt buckle didn't feel so lucky anymore.

Chapter 17
The Big Day

MY DAD AND I PULLED into the arena parking lot at eight o'clock on the dot. Already, the place was filling up with horse and stock trailers. I saw Scotty across the lot helping his dad unload cattle for the events. He was too busy with an ornery calf to see me, though. All around men and women were unloading their horses and tying them to hitches, saddling them, rubbing them down, or combing their manes and tails.

The smell of saddle soap and horses filled the air as my dad and I started getting ready, too.

"You better get over there to register," Dad said. "I'll finish up here."

I nodded and took off running towards the office. Cecil and Bo were just coming out the door as I got there.

"What's the arena look like?" I asked them.

"Muddy," Bo said.

"I figured," I said. "Many registered yet?"

"Quite a few," Cecil said. "Lot of out-of-towners."

"I figured," I said. "I'll catch you later."

"Good luck," Bo offered. Cecil gave a nod in agreement.

"You, too," I said.

I was thinking after they left that they were cordial but not as friendly as they used to be. It was like a wedge had been driven between us and I couldn't budge it. I didn't have much time to stew over it, because I was next in line to register. After that, I was too busy warming up Checkers and focusing on my event to think about anything else.

Calf-roping came up pretty quick. I waited in the pre-event corral with the other contenders, including Bo, Cecil, and Scotty, who were ahead of me in the line-up.

All I could think about was getting to that calf quick without breaking the barrier rope. The barrier rope stretches across the starting box, the place where Checkers and I go when it is our turn to compete. The barrier allows the calf a head start. Breaking it would add ten seconds to my score, which would surely put me out of the running.

Checkers had a jumpy edge to him this morning, even after our warm-up, and I was praying that he would wait for my signal before taking off after the calf. As a rule, I usually wait till the calf's shoulder gets to the gate before signaling. With the muddy conditions of the arena, the calf might stumble, which would slow him down, and I might come out too fast, especially with the way Checkers was chomping at the bit to get going.

Scotty was first to go. He rode Paint into the box, turned, and faced forward. I could see he kept his eye on the calf in the chute, waiting for the calf to quit fighting against it. Scotty nodded, signaling for them to open the gate.

The calf stumbled leaving the chute, then took off across the arena. Scotty had played it safe and waited a split second longer than usual to give Paint the signal. But once he gave it to him, Paint took off like a shot. Scotty drew close enough to the calf's left hip for Paint to rate the calf, and with Paint and the calf running at the same speed, he threw his loop. It wrapped clean.

He jerked the slack in his right hand so he could spin the calf rather than knock him over backwards.

Soon as Paint stopped dead in his tracks, holding that calf taut, Scotty jumped off Paint and slid down the rope, grabbed the calf, and flipped him on his side.

He took his piggin' string, the shorter, skinnier rope that he held in his teeth, and grabbed the top front leg. But when he went to wrap the piggin' string around it, the calf squirmed out of his grasp and wriggled to its feet. One of the arena cowboys undid the rope from the calf's neck. Scotty got up on Paint and rode to the far gate; his shoulders slumped.

Bo and Ranger went next. Bo signaled he was ready with a nod, but instead of his usual clean and fast run, he broke the barrier, failing to give his calf the head start the rules required. Ten seconds was added to his score, enough to disqualify him from the final rounds. He knew it, too. The way he cocked his head, with his chin down, gave him away.

Cecil made a good clean start, but Rocket stumbled in the mud, nearly throwing him from the saddle. Cecil clung on and kept going. Rocket rated the calf, and as his horse kept pace with the calf, running with it like it was its own shadow, Cecil swung his loop, wrapping the calf's neck.

He jerked the slack, pulled it, and jumped to the muddy ground, slipping and sliding over to the calf, his left hand reaching for its neck. He bent his knees into the calf's side, grabbed its right flank, lifted, and the calf rolled over. He and the calf were both breathing hard as he tied the calf's feet with two wraps and a half hitch.

Cecil remounted Rocket and nudged him forward to loosen the tension on the rope, waited that long six seconds, praying the piggin' string would hold.

You could tell when he saw the signal, 'cause his whole body relaxed. It was a clean run! The crowd broke into applause.

80

The arena cowboy untied the calf, and the calf jumped to its feet. He led the calf on the end of his rope down to the opposite end of the arena and out through another gate. I saw Cecil give Rocket a firm pat on the neck; it was his way of telling the horse he had done a good job. But from the way he pranced out of the arena, Rocket already knew that. Cecil's score was not as good as usual, but he was still in the running.

I was next. I backed Checkers into the box and decided, after seeing how jumpy the calves ahead of me had been, that I was going to hold Checkers back till the calf's hip reached a spot a few feet out of the chute before giving Checkers the signal.

I gripped my piggin' string tight in my teeth, my catch-rope looped in my hand. Once the calf quit fighting the chute I nodded for the release. The gate opened and the calf took off.

Checkers's muscles tensed, ready to run, but I held him back a few seconds longer before squeezing him with my legs as hard as I could. Checkers sprang forward out of the box. I rode the stirrups, urging him to go faster till he pulled up behind the calf, rating him.

I swung my rope, making the loop bigger and bigger, then tossed the loop, following through with my arm and hand pointing to where I wanted the loop to land. It missed the calf's head.

I threw my second rope, but it missed, too.

The calf ran to the far gate.

The feeling of disappointment that came over me couldn't have been worse, or so I thought.

Then Checkers and I exited the arena and I saw Jack and Bart waving me over to them. They had already gathered up the other Bulldoggers.

Things were about to get worse.

"Well, it's like this." Jack reached out his gloved hand and turned it palm up. There sat one of the nastiest, pointiest, dried-out cockleburs I had ever seen.

"What are those for?" Bo asked.

"Good question," Jack said. "You see those two hicks standing over there, the ones with the scarves tied round their necks?"

"Yeah . . ." Cecil said, slowly. I could tell by the drag in his voice that he knew what was coming and he didn't like it one bit.

"They're getting ready to make their runs, and right before they do, we want you to find a way to stick these under their saddle blankets."

Cecil started kicking clumps of mud hard with his boot, sending mud clods flying in all directions. I glanced at Bo and Scotty; their faces were red as beets.

"How do you expect us to do that?" I asked, stalling for time.

Cecil balled his hands into fists. He was getting madder by the minute. Jack and Bart were asking us to go against the cowboy code, and that could only end badly.

"Find a way to distract them and then plant these sweet critters where it'll bite," Bart said.

"That'd be cheating," Bo said.

"Don't strain your brain trying to think, moron," Jack told Bo.

I was beginning to get steamed at the way he was talking to Bo. But it was Cecil who I was most worried about. He hadn't taken his eyes off the ground, and he was still just a'kicking those mud clumps to dust. And then he stopped and looked at Jack square in the face.

"You have a lot of nerve, talking to Bo like that," Cecil said. "What's more, you have fish guts for brains if you think we're going to rig the deal and risk being disqualified."

"Besides, it's just wrong!" Bo chimed in.

"I think they're chicken," Bart taunted.

"No. They're plumb stupid," Jack said through clenched teeth.

"We're neither," Cecil said. "You can go find yourself some-

Chapter 18
The Last Straw

I DECIDED MY BEST BET was to take my time. No need to rush. I dismounted Checkers, loosened the cinches on his saddle, and walked him around until he cooled down, before tying him to a fence rail. I turned then, looking for my dad. I coiled my rope around my arm and tried to see if I had imagined the two menaces. Nope, it was no mirage.

Dad, who was normally waiting for me when I came out of the arena after a run, was nowhere to be found. I hooked my rope over the saddle horn and strode towards Jack and Bart, trying to appear sure of myself, though I was having a hard time convincing myself I was tough, much less anyone else.

"We've another job for you boys," Jack said.

Scotty started to protest, but Bart scowled at him and Scotty backed down.

"You boys done such a fine job picking trash that we thought you might like to do something a little more fun," Jack said.

"What could be more fun than picking trash?" I asked.

one else to extort. You're not getting anything else from us—I don't care what you threaten to do to us."

Extort? Where'd he come up with that word, I wondered. I didn't even know he knew what it meant; he must have been watching "Law & Order" again.

Jack walked up to Cecil and started poking Cecil's chest with his finger. Hard.

"You better do as you're told, or else."

"Or else what?" Cecil said, in an in-your-face sort of way.

"Or else we'll grind you down so all that'll be sticking out of this mud here will be the tops of your heads. That's what."

"I'd like to see you try."

Cecil spat the words at him and raised his fists as if preparing to take the two of them on.

In that moment I realized there was no way we could handle those two bulldozers. They had more than five years and two hundred pounds on us. But we also weren't going to help them cheat.

"Cops!!" I yelled, and pointed behind Jack and Bart.

Jack and Bart turned and looked over their shoulders. It was all the time we needed; the four of us took off running.

By the time Jack and Bart figured out my ploy and started after us, we had a good head start.

"Meet at the clubhouse!" I yelled.

We split up, each going in a different direction. The last time I looked behind me. Jack was running full stride after Cecil. And then I saw Bart, and, well, he was coming after me, like I was someone from the opposite team carrying the ball to the goal and he wasn't about to let me score.

Chapter 19
The Getaway

ONLY ONE THING KEPT going through my mind as I ran: *I am dead as a dodo if I don't shake Bart from my tail.* He might be none to smart, but there's no doubt why they made him an end on the football team: He could run faster and farther than anyone at Bootleg High, even if he did occasionally get turned around and score for the opposing team.

Because the arena was on the north side of town, I had to cut across Main Street, go through town, and then take the highway to get home. Or I could cut across and through the fields east of town and work my way west to the highway and home. *But if I go into town there is more to slow me down,* I argued with myself. *If I take to the fields, I can lose him for sure. But to throw Bart off track, I'll have to make him lose sight of me.* Running laps was coming in handy so far as making a getaway, but my short legs were no match for Bart's long ones.

I could hear his big feet slapping the ground behind me, his heavy breaths coming faster and closer. I dared a look behind me and I swear he was so close I could see the gap between his two front teeth. He dove for me and his hands brushed the sleeve of my shirt. I sidestepped out of reach; he hit the ground with a thud.

Across Mrs. Colby's yard I saw the door to her shed was open, and it gave me an idea. I turned on my heel and headed straight for it. But when I reached it, instead of going inside, I slammed the door to the shed hard, so hard Bart had to hear it, and then I ran and hid around back. Just as I had hoped, Bart came running up to the shed door.

"Got you now," I heard him say.

The door squeaked as he opened it.

I had already sneaked around to the other side of the building, where I had hunkered down out of view. Through a small window, I watched and waited, listening and looking for Bart to step inside. A shadow appeared at the doorway, then Bart's square head poked through.

"Where'd you go?" Bart growled.

He was having trouble making out things in the dark shed.

One more step, I said to myself, *just take one more step* . . .

"I knows you're in there, hick," Bart said.

And then he walked right into my trap.

I ran around front, slammed the door to the shed, and latched it. As I passed by the window, I couldn't resist giving the pane a little rap with my knuckles. When Bart saw me I smiled and waved. The look on his face was definitely a Kodak moment. Too bad I didn't have my camera.

Figuring someone would hear him hollering and set him free—but not till I was out of sight and too far away for him to follow me—I took off.

I ran all the way to the storm cellar, anyway.

When the clubhouse came in sight, I hid in the thick brush along the highway till I was sure no one had seen me. Slowly, I made my way to the cellar, fighting the urge to make a run for it, careful not to make a racket. A rustling sound off to my left stopped me in my tracks. It might have been Jack, but it could also have been one of the Bulldoggers.

Luckily, one of the first things we did when we started the club was come up with a secret call, but I had to wonder if they would recognize it, since this would be the first official time it had been used. It was worth a try.

I whistled three times, mimicking the unique, two-syllable call of a quail.

"Bob-white, bob-white, bob-white."

I held my breath, listening, waiting.

Nothing. I tried again.

"Bob-white, bob-white, bob-white."

When still no one answered, I figured I was the first one to get to the fraidy hole.

Chapter 20
A Reality Check

SCOTTY!" I EXCLAIMED. I had opened the door to the cellar expecting to see no one, only to find Scotty inside, standing knee-deep in rainwater.

"Hey, Dru! Where are the others?"

"I don't know," I said. "If they're not here, they should be right behind us."

"Yeah, I hope so."

I climbed down into the storm shelter with Scotty. The water was cold and slimy with mud and smelled like rotting leaves. I closed the door behind me just to be on the safe side, and we stood there, knowing the other was there, but in the pitch dark of the cellar, I couldn't see my hand in front of my face, much less Scotty.

I heard a creak and the door opened. Daylight streamed in. My heart bumped hard in my chest, until I realized it was Bo, with Cecil following close behind. They climbed down to where we were and closed the door.

"Where's Jack?" I asked.

"Lost him about half a mile back," Cecil said. "You know that prairie dog village near town? Well, I came running through there with Jack on my tail. Last I saw him he had stepped in one of them holes. That burrow laid him out flat."

"This cellar doesn't make for such a good clubhouse when it rains," Bo said, splashing about in the dark.

"It stinks in here, too," Cecil added.

"You're not kidding," I said.

"I've gone and ripped my lucky jeans, running through those sticker bushes," Bo said.

"That's just a superstition," Scotty said. "Those pants aren't really lucky."

"You don't know everything," Bo said. "The day that bull tossed my dad in the dirt, he wasn't wearing his lucky hat, and look what happened."

"That might've happened anyway. You can't say it was wearing or not wearing that hat that caused it," Scotty argued.

"Leave him alone," I said.

"Don't tell me what to do," Scotty said. "If it weren't for your swelled head over that catfish we wouldn't be in this mess in the first place. As far as I'm concerned, I don't think this club is such a good idea anymore."

"Yeah, we're sitting in this bucket of water you call a clubhouse missing the final rounds," Bo piped up. "I think it's a sign."

"A sign of what?" I asked. I was beginning to think maybe these were the things Scotty had been wanting to talk about a couple of days ago.

"Like maybe this club isn't such a good idea," Bo said. "We haven't had a moment's peace since we started it."

"Cecil's the only one who had a decent run," Scotty added. "If we'd practiced more . . ."

"Hold on a minute, are you all saying you want to dissolve The Bulldoggers Club?" I gulped. "You want to quit?"

"Maybe."

I wasn't sure who had said it, it was so dark in the cellar, but I felt it could have been any one of them the way things were going.

"But I thought we were tight!" I said.

My fellow Bulldoggers didn't make a peep, each hoping, I could tell, that one of the others would say something first.

Finally, Cecil spoke up.

"Dru, the idea of the club was a good one," he said, "but I think they're right. None of us have been acting much like buds."

"I think what you meant to say was that I hadn't been acting like we were buds," I said. "And you're absolutely right. I'm the one who started all this trouble and I'm the one who has to fix it."

"How're you going to do that?" Cecil asked. "Jack and Bart are sure to kill us next time they see us."

I thought back to what my dad had said about dealing with trouble, and I knew what I had to do to make things right.

"My dad told me the best way out of trouble is always through it," I said. "I wasn't sure what that meant at first, but now I think I've figured out what he was saying. I am going to have to tell Tug where we caught that fish."

"But we're all going to get into trouble then," Cecil said.

"More trouble than what we've been in?" Scotty asked.

"Yeah, once it's out in the open, Jack and Bart won't have nothing on us," Bo said.

"Exactly," I said.

"But we got something on them," Cecil said. "Remember that day we caught the fish? We caught them two smoking."

"I'd forgotten about that," Scotty said.

"We should treat them like they've been treating us," Cecil said. I could hear the smile in his voice.

"Naw, we don't want to stoop to their level," Scotty said.

"My dad always says, give them enough rope and they'll hang themselves," Bo said. "Let's just wait and see."

"So, Dru," Cecil said, "what're you saying?"

"I'm saying that I don't want us to split up our club. If you give me another chance, I'll make things right."

"I move that we give Dru another chance," Cecil said, and slapped the water with the finality of a judge wielding his gavel.

"All agreed, say 'yup,' " he added.

"Yup," Bo and Scotty said.

"Now," Scotty said, "let's get the heck out of this fraidy hole, what did Bo call it? Oh yeah, this 'bucket of water.' I'm freezing my toes off!"

Chapter 21
Cash Goes Missing

B Y THE TIME THE FOUR of us Bulldoggers made it back to the rodeo arena, our clothes had dried out, but we still smelled like fresh manure. To my surprise, the parking lot was nearly empty.

"Hey, where is everybody?" Cecil said.

"My dad's pickup's gone," I said, "but he left Checkers here. That's weird."

"Something's wrong," Bo said.

"Yeah," Scotty said. "There's Miss Lucy. She'll know what's going on."

We ran over to Miss Lucy's concession stand. Her nose crinkled up as we grouped around the ordering window.

"Oh, boy," she said, reaching up to pinch her nose closed. "You boys are ripe."

"Miss Lucy," I said, "what's going on? Where'd everybody go after the roping finished?"

"Where have you been? I don't know how you could've missed

all the excitement," she said. "That young feller, Cash, is missing."

"What happened?" I asked.

"Well, his mom said that after school yesterday he told her he was going fishing . . . and he never came back."

"Since yesterday?" I asked.

"Yup. This morning the sheriff came in after his men searched all night. Made an announcement over the loudspeaker that he needed folks to help with the search. They all just lit out of here; I'd say not more than an hour ago."

"Where were they headed?" Scotty asked.

"Well, you know, it's a sad thing, but the sheriff said he was afraid the boy had gone over that waterfall and drowned, like that Harlin boy. You know how everyone's been making fools of themselves trying to break your record, Dru, so bound and determined to catch themselves a monster catfish. Going to be a sad day for us all if the sheriff's right."

"We have to go help with the search," I said, remembering my conversation with Cash on the school bus.

"Let's go a'horseback," Bo said.

"Good idea!" Scotty said.

We each ran and untied our horses, mounted up, and kicked our horses into a gallop. As we rode across town to the highway, I recalled Cash's puzzled expression when I told him where I had caught that fish, like he didn't believe me. *Could he have known the truth*, I wondered. *But how? Jack and Bart were the only ones who knew where we'd caught that catfish. Or were they?*

When we reached the south side of town we urged our horses to go faster, afraid for Cash, afraid for his mom worrying about him.

"Let's take the short cut," I said to the others. "We'll cut across Winterhalter Creek at my place!"

If Cash knew the truth behind our record catfish haul, no wonder they couldn't find him at the waterfall. The more I thought about it, the harder I kept pushing Checkers to go faster across the fields dotted with cattle. As we crossed the creek bed, the four of us side by side, I realized, like a knife to the chest, just how much trouble one little lie could cause. If I had told the truth from the get-go, well, we probably would've been given a good talking-to, and probably grounded to boot, but we wouldn't have had to do the dumb stunts those two helmet-heads Jack and Bart had made us do. More than that, Cash wouldn't be missing now.

Once we crossed the creek, we followed it till we came to Nurse Blanchett's place.

"This way, guys," I said. "I bet I know where Cash is."

"Quicksand Pond?" Scotty asked. "Why there?"

"Just a hunch," I said.

"What do you mean a hunch?" Cecil said.

"You're going to have to trust me on this one," I said.

Bo, Cecil, and Scotty looked at each other.

"Why should we?" Cecil asked.

"You got good reason not to, but it'll take too long to explain."

"I just hope you're right," Cecil said.

"Me, too. Are you with me?"

They nodded. We followed the same path we had taken before, the day we caught the monster catfish. We found a break in the fence to lead our horses through. The catfish skeletons and coyote skulls hanging on Nurse Blanchett's fence were even spookier this time around, what with us already thinking about Cash missing, laying hurt somewhere, or worse, dead. We came up over a small rise and the pond came in view. We reined in our horses and scanned the shoreline of the pond, looking for Cash.

"I don't see anything," Bo said.

"Me, neither," Cecil said.

"Wait," I said. "He could be lying real still somewhere."

We looked again, but we still didn't see Cash.

"Let's go on down," I said. "He has to be here."

We urged our horses into motion, searching the nearby fields, the yard and garden, and back to the pond again.

"Over there! What's that?" I yelled. "Do you see it? On the

other side of the pond, by that dead tree in the water?"

Sure enough it was Cash, holding onto what was left of that dead tree for dear life. He had got himself in one quicksand pickle.

We rode down the hill and as we drew closer, I could hear Cash hollering at us. He took one hand from around the tree trunk to wave us over, but his other stayed clasping it like a vice.

From the chest down, he was mired in quicksand. And it looked like he had lost his glasses.

"You two," I said, pointing at Bo and Scotty, "ride over to the waterfall for more help, while Cecil and I do what we can here."

"Sure enough," Bo said.

Scotty agreed with a nod. They turned Paint and Ranger on their heels and took off like they was breaking out of the box at the state roping finals. Meanwhile Cecil and I rode around the pond closer to where Cash was stuck.

"Hang on, Cash! We'll think of something," Cecil said.

"I can't hold on much longer," Cash said, his voice trembling.

"You've held on this long," I called to him. "You can hold on a little longer."

I turned to Cecil.

"Look, he's probably not going to be able to hold on to this rope, but if we could get it around him, he might be able to slip it under his arms, and I bet we could pull him out between the two of us."

"That's what I was thinking, too."

"You're the better roper. Why don't you give it a try."

Cecil took his catch-rope and started swinging it.

"Cash, listen. Cecil's going to toss his loop over you. All you have to do is get it down under one arm. We'll be able to pull you out with no trouble. You won't have to do nothing but keep your chin up."

Cash nodded. He looked like he wanted to cry.

"Okay, Cecil. Give it a go."

By now Cecil had the loop a good size, and he was a'swinging it over his head. Finally, he let it loose. The loop sailed over the water. It fell a few feet short of Cash. Cecil reeled it back in and started again, swinging it over his head, making the loop bigger and bigger. He tossed it again.

The loop floated on the light breeze across the water towards Cash and when it came down it encircled his head and shoulders, like a life buoy, just as it was supposed to.

"Put your arm through, Cash!" I hollered. "Nod when you're ready!"

Cash hooked his arm through the loop and nodded.

"Okay, Cecil, here we go," I said.

We both took hold of the end of the rope and pulled till the slack disappeared.

"You have to let go of the tree, Cash . . . come on, let go!"

"I can't," Cash cried.

"You have to!" Cecil called.

"I can't let go," he called back. "My arm's frozen."

"I guess his arm muscles have cramped from holding on so long. Now what?" I asked Cecil.

"One of us has to go out there," Cecil said. "If I go, will you be able to pull us both out?"

"No, but Checkers and I could," I said.

"That'll work," he said.

"Okay, Cash, Cecil's going to come out to help you free your arm, then Checkers and I will pull you both out."

Cash nodded to show he understood.

Cecil walked over to the downed tree. The exposed roots stuck out like a bad hair cut, thick and gnarled; the tree's trunk and stunted branches, what was left of them, leaned towards the pond. Cecil grabbed a'hold of one of the roots and began climbing out towards Cash. He was probably doing exactly what Cash had done to get into this mess in the first place.

The way I figured it Cash must have either slipped off trying to get out on the end of the fallen tree trunk to fish or been standing on the tree trunk fishing and lost his balance and fallen—dropping right into the quicksand. Luckily he had managed to grab onto the tree trunk as he fell and then hung on for dear life.

Once Cecil climbed over the roots to the base of the tree, he stood and inched his way down the length of the trunk out over the water, before pausing and creeping out closer to Cash. I held tight to my end of the rope wrapped around Cash's waist until Cecil lowered himself down beside him.

"Give me a little slack!" Cecil yelled to me.

I did, and Cecil enlarged the loop of the rope so that it fit around both of them now.

I could see Cecil talking to Cash as he tried to free his arm.

"Okay," Cecil called to me.

I tightened the slack of the rope and tied it hard and fast around Checkers's saddle horn.

"Okay, boy . . . back."

Checkers's ears perked up as he went into action, slowly backing away from the pond with Cash and Cecil in tow, a big sucking sound let me know the pond was releasing them.

"Good boy, good boy," I said to Checkers. "Keep going . . . you're doing great."

I kept my eyes on Cash and Cecil as the rope dragged them out of the quicksand and across to the shore.

When Cecil got close enough to get a foothold, he picked up Cash and carried him to the bank and laid him down. Cash was wet and shivering. I took off my shirt and wrapped it around him.

It was time to get some answers.

"Cash," I said, "how'd you know we caught that fish here?"

He shook his head, as if he didn't want to answer my question.

"It's okay. I won't get mad or nothing."

"The truth is I followed you guys out here that day."

"Where were you?"

"I was hiding over there, behind that old out building."

I looked across the way, to where he was pointing.

Chapter 22
Making Things right

DOC HAZNOTT WAS THE first to reach us, with the sheriff behind him. Cecil and I stepped aside to let the adults take care of Cash. As good as it felt to have Cash safe and sound on solid ground, I knew my dad would be none too pleased when he learned it was all my fault. *Never mind about that*, I told myself. *A man's got to do what a man's got to do.*

As soon as I saw Dad's pickup pull up and he jumped out of the cab, I thought I had better just get it over with. He was all smiles and congratulations, but I stopped his approach with my hand held up like a crossing guard stopping traffic.

"Dad," I said, my tone serious. "This is not what it looks like. I'm no hero."

"What're you talking about, son? You boys just saved Cash's life," he said.

"No sir, it's my fault he was in the quicksand. He never would've gone to Quicksand Pond if I had told the truth in the first place."

"Told the truth about what?"

I swallowed hard.

"I never caught that catfish at the waterfall. I caught it right here in Nurse Blanchett's pond."

My dad's smiled disappeared, but before he could say a word, I heard someone shuffle up beside us. Seems Nurse Blanchett had come out to see why people were milling about her property, when she overheard my dad and I talking.

"What's this I hear?" Nurse Blanchett said gruffly, as she came and stood beside my dad.

My knees started to shake at the sight of her.

"I'm sorry Ms. Blanchett, but we came over and fished in your pond while you were away," I said to her, meekly. "But the worst part is that I lied about where I caught the catfish so no one would know, and I have been lying about everything, it seems like, ever since!"

I lowered my eyes to regain my strength.

And then the story just spilled out.

"Bo, here, why, he didn't think twice about helping me when I got stuck in the quicksand that day we caught the fish. He saved my life. And he caught the bluegill I used as bait—don't think that catfish would have ever have taken that puny worm I started with.

"And Cecil and Scotty, why, once I hooked her and got her to shore, they helped keep her there. And then bringing it home, everybody helped to carry her. Bo gave the shirt off his back to keep that fish from getting torn to pieces on barbed wire and thorns. I never should've taken all the credit for her like that.

"But then Jack and Bart made us pick up trash along the highway or else they said they would tell everybody the truth and I lied about that, too, and the lie just kept getting bigger.

"And then everybody was trying to catch a record-breaker like ours, and Cash having seen where we *really* caught her tried to go and catch a bigger one.

"And the guys got mad at me for hogging all the glory. None

of it would have happened if I'd been honest in the first place.

"But the worst part of it is that I let everybody down, including myself, and I'm sorry."

Nurse Blanchett and my dad just stood there stunned.

Finally, Nurse Blanchett spoke.

"Dru, I can tell you feel bad about you and your friends trespassing on my land. What's so sad, is none of this had to happen. I would have been happy to give you permission to fish in the pond, if you had just asked."

I couldn't believe what I was hearing, but my dad was standing there, nodding in agreement.

"We used to fish there all the time back when I was in school," my dad said. "Of course, we knew enough to ask permission first."

Before I could respond, a crowd gathered around us. And when I came up for air, they broke out clapping, though I didn't deserve no clapping given what I had done.

The applause only made me feel worse, thinking about how selfish I had been, how wrong I'd been about Nurse Blanchett, and how I'd almost lost the best friends a guy could have.

"I just want to go home," I said, turning to my dad.

"Okay, son," he said. "Let's go."

And he took me and Checkers home.

Chapter 23
Official Business

SOMETIMES ALL A GUY needs is a good cry. And I am not too proud to admit to crying from time to time. That night, my dad sat with me on my bed and we had a long talk about things, about what it takes to make a man. Hard work, for one. Honesty, for another. And courage. The courage to face up to your own shortcomings. The courage to do what's right and proper, even when it's hard. The courage to cry if you need to.

Once we finished our talk, I started feeling lighter, like somebody had taken a big ole load off me. Dad told me he thought I had grown some over the course of the past week, and not just taller, either.

Sunday, after church, Dad went with me to talk to Tug about the fish tale I had told. Turns out we still had a record catfish, just in a different category. Overall Tug took the news well, said we boys had made his bait shop famous. People from all corners of the state were coming to have their picture taken with him in front of the shop.

After we left Tug's, Dad and I went to see Nurse Blanchett. I guess chopping wood for a month of Saturdays at her place isn't too bad a punishment when you consider all the trouble I caused.

Next we stopped by home and emptied all that frozen catfish from our freezer, loaded it in the pickup, and then drove around giving it to all those folks who ride the church van to service. You should've seen their faces when we handed them enough catfish for a month of Sunday dinners.

We made one more stop before we went home, that was to Bo's, to drop off the newly bought shirt and blue jeans I had gotten for him with my own money to replace the ones he gave up for our misadventure.

. . . .

Monday, after school, Cecil called an official meeting of The Bulldoggers Club, and he insisted we meet someplace other than the storm cellar. He suggested the bleachers at the high school track, mumbling something about that working until we could find a new clubhouse.

I didn't take it personal. If standing water and spiders weren't bad enough, the cellar now held too many bad memories for me to want to hang out there.

When the bell rang to signal the end of school, I hightailed it to the track, but Bo, Cecil, and Scotty were already there.

As I walked up the bleachers to join the guys, Cecil waved to someone across the football field. I turned and saw Cash running as fast as he could up to where we were.

Cecil called the meeting to order. I didn't take offense. I might have been president of the club, but I was a president in disgrace. Instead of banging a gavel, Cecil handed out a piece of bubble gum to each of us as the first order of business.

A peace-offering, I thought.

"Okay," Cecil said, between popping his gum, "I called this

104

meeting for three reasons, Dru. First of all, we wanted to ask you if you still wanted to be president of the club, seeing as how you set everything straight, and all?"

"You bet!" I looked around the group. "Does this mean we're not going to dissolve the The Bulldoggers Club?"

Bo, Cecil, and Scotty broke into broad grins.

"Yup!" they said.

I looked over at Cash and smiled.

"My first order of business then, as president, is to recommend Cash as our newest member of The Bulldoggers Club. All agreed?"

Bo, Cecil, and Scotty's grins grew bigger.

"Yup!" they said.

"Okay, Cash, you are now an official Bulldogger."

"Cool," Cash said, pushing his new glasses back up his nose.

"Next we got to find ourselves a new clubhouse," I said. "Anybody got any ideas?"

"Someplace dry," Bo said.

"Someplace above ground," Scotty said.

"Someplace without scorpions," Cecil chimed in.

Everybody seconded that last one.

"What about the hayloft in our barn?" I suggested.

"That'd be perfect," Cecil said.

Scotty, Bo, and Cash agreed by high-fiving each other.

"That's settled then," I said.

"Mister President," Cecil interrupted, "the second reason we called this meeting is because the Bulldoggers have decided we aren't going to let you chop wood all by yourself."

"But you guys picked up trash for a whole week," I argued. "You wouldn't have had to do that if I had just told the truth from the start."

"No buts," Cecil said. "We could have told the truth ourselves, but we didn't. Anyway, we're Bulldoggers. We're in this together."

The other members nodded agreement.

"And third," Cecil said, "there was something we wanted you to see, and it should be showing up here any minute."

He pointed across the track.

"Here they come!"

I looked up to see Jack and Bart running onto the track with Coach right behind them.

"Coach found cigarettes in their lockers," Cecil explained. "They get to run laps during baseball practice for the next week."

"Tell him what else those two jerks have to do," Bo said, smiling big.

"No, you can tell him," Cecil said.

"Well, once the judge found out they had been pushing all their chores onto us, he gave them another sixty days of community service."

"You're kidding," I said. "Well, I'll be."

"You haven't heard the best part yet," Bo said. "Seems the judge's grandson is a calf roper. He was the one they wanted us to mess with. They'll be cleaning the rodeo grounds after every event this season to boot."

"Those hotshots got themselves knee-deep in horse manure, any way you look at it," Scotty said.

"What goes around comes around," I said.

And I ought'a know.

Bulldogger Lingo

(and terms)

a'horseback: riding a horse

American Quarter Horse: also known as a quarter horse : any of a breed of stocky muscular horses capable of high speed for short distances : since 1940 the official name of a breed used to work cattle on ranches and compete in timed rodeo events : most often sorrel (brownish red), there are sixteen other recognized colors of this breed

Bill Pickett: an African-American-Cherokee cowboy from Texas, recognized by two halls of fame as the sole inventor of bulldogging, or steer wrestling, the only rodeo event that can be attributed to a single individual : his unique method of bulldogging steers involved jumping from his horse to a steer's back, biting the steer's upper lip, and throwing the steer to the ground by its horns

barrier rope: the rope that stretches across the starting box in a calf-roping event

bluegill: an edible North American freshwater fish of the sunfish family, closely related to the perch : popular with anglers : sometimes used as bait for catfish : a nongame fish

bulldogger: also steer wrestler : one who wrestles steers

bulldogging: also steer wrestling : a rodeo event in which a cowboy jumps from his horse, grabs a steer by the horns, and flips him over onto the ground while being timed

catch-rope: a rope used to lasso steers and whatnot

catfish: a freshwater or marine fish with whisker-like barbels around the mouth, typically bottom-dwelling : in the state of Oklahoma a game fish

chute: a passage through which the calf is released into the arena during a roping competition

cow-tipping: rural legend : the act of sneaking up on a sleeping, standing cow and pushing it over for a prank : possible in certain instances but not probable, as cattle, unlike horses, do not sleep standing up but dose and are easily disturbed : a recent study found it would take 2,910 Newtons of force to topple an average cow, the equivalent of 4.43 people

Cross Timbers: a twenty- to thirty-mile-wide strip of land in the United States that runs from southeastern Kansas across central Oklahoma to central Texas : made up of a mix of prairie, savanna, and woodland, it marks the western habitat limit of many mammals and insects and contains many post oak and blackjack oak in coarse, sandy soils

dually: a pickup truck, specifically one with four wheels on the rear axle

noodling: catching fish barehanded

quarter horse: any of a breed of stocky muscular horses capable of high speed for short distances

rate the calf: when horse and the calf are running at the same speed

riding the stirrups: standing in stirrups while horse is moving

rodeo: from the Spanish *rodear*, which means "to surround" or "go around" : first used in American English in 1834 to denote a "round up" of cattle : later a public event featuring sixteen events, of which six were contests, including cowboy bareback and saddle bronc riding, cowgirl bronc riding, steer riding, steer wrestling, and calf roping : today a public event that usually features three to four timed events

rodeo clown: a rodeo performer in clown garb who works in bull riding and other rodeo competitions, whose job is to protect a rider from the bull once the rider has been bucked off or has jumped off the animal

starting box: where ropers wait for the calf to come out'a the chute

steer wrestler: also bulldoggers : one who wrestles steers

steer wrestling: also bulldogging : a rodeo event in which a cowboy jumps from his horse, grabs a steer by the horns, and flips him over onto the ground while being timed

storm cellar: also known as a fraidy hole : an underground shelter where you can go until a storm passes : underground shelter used to avoid being sucked up by a tornado and flung to Kingdom Come

stringer: metal stake attached to a string used to carry a mess of freshly caught fish

tack: equipment used in horseback riding, including the saddle and bridle

tack room: a room, often in a barn or out building, where saddles and other gear for horseback riding, including saddle blankets, ropes, chaps, bridles, and bits, are stored

two wraps and a half hitch: the knot used to tie a calf's feet together after it has been bulldogged in a roping event

Easy Baked Catfish

 1 **freshly caught catfish, 2-3 pounds, filleted**
   Water
2-3 **tablespoons of salt for soaking**
 1 **whole lemon, sliced**
1/4 **cup olive oil or melted butter**
1-2 **teaspoons salt***
 2 **teaspoons pepper***
   Aluminum foil

> ** add more or less according to your taste—you can always add more later but you can't remove it once it is in!*

Fill a medium to large bowl with enough water to cover the catfish. Stir in two to three tablespoons of salt. Add the fillets and soak for 30 minutes (catfish are bottom-feeders so if you don't, your fillets will taste muddy).

Place fillets in a piece of aluminum foil (large enough to wrap all the fish and still seal at the top). Drizzle half of the olive oil or butter over the top side of the fillets. Sprinkle each fillet with half of the salt and the pepper. Flip fillets and repeat last two steps. Spread lemon slices on top of seasoned fillets.

Bring both sides of foil up and seal by folding edges together. Place packet with fish on a baking sheet. Preheat oven to 375 degrees F.; bake fillets at 375 degrees F. until interior of fish is 150 degrees F. (If you don't have a meat thermometer cook the fish until the fillet turns opaque. Catfish does not flake easily when done, like trout or bass, so the size or amount of catfish you are cooking will determine the length of cooking time needed. For safety's sake, it is best to use a meat thermometer.)

Options: You can change up the recipe by cutting a medium white onion into rings and laying the onion rings on top of the fillets instead of the lemon slices. Or you can substitute either Cajun or Creole seasoning for the lemon, salt, and pepper.

Yield: Will serve a family of four. A serving is about 3 1/2 ounces, about the size of a deck of playing cards. (One serving of catfish provides almost half of a person's total daily protein requirement.)

Acknowledgements

I would like to thank Bill Hale, assistant chief of law enforcement at the Oklahoma Department of Wildlife, for his help with fishing rules and regulations in Oklahoma, especially as they pertain to channel catfish and state fishing records.

A big thank you also to author John R. Erickson, whose book on lariats, *Catch Rope: The Long Arm of the Cowboy*, I found to be both great reading and informative with regards to catch-ropes.

The opening quote from Oklahoma humorist Will Rogers is word perfect thanks to the help of Jennifer Holt, curator of collections for the Will Rogers Memorial Museum in Claremore.

A heartfelt thanks also to Dick Lewis of Ponca City, a farrier and horseman, who shared with me some of his own childhood stories of growing up in rural Oklahoma. Thanks Dick for reading and commenting on the first draft of this book. Your wisdom and suggestions are greatly appreciated.

About the Author

Barbara Hay is also the author of the young adult novel *Lesson of the White Eagle* (The RoadRunner Press, October 2011). Her work has appeared in the Tulsa World, *Columbia* magazine, the Sooner Catholic, and *Women's World*. She holds a bachelor's degree in liberal studies from the University of Oklahoma. The widowed mother of four children, she lives and writes in Oklahoma. Visit her at www.BarbaraHay.com.